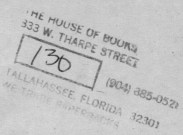
"Healing was respected in my age," Parsons said. "But you people seem to think it's somehow wrong."

A furious rustle leaped through the circle of listeners.

"Wrong!" Stenog snapped. "It's madness! Don't you see what would happen if everybody were healed? All the sick and injured? The old?"

"No wonder his society collapsed," a harsh-eyed girl said.

Berkley books by Philip K. Dick

THE COSMIC PUPPETS
DR. FUTURITY
THE MAN IN THE HIGH CASTLE
THE UNTELEPORTED MAN

PHILIP K. DICK
DR·FUTURITY

BERKLEY BOOKS, NEW YORK

DR. FUTURITY

A Berkley Book / published by arrangement with
the author's estate

PRINTING HISTORY
Previously published by Ace Books.
Berkley edition / August 1984

ISBN: 0-425-07106-5

A BERKLEY BOOK® TM 757,375
Berkley Books are published by The Berkley Publishing Group,
200 Madison Avenue, New York, N.Y. 10016.
The name "BERKLEY" and the stylized "B" with design are
trademarks belonging to Berkley Publishing Corporation.
PRINTED IN THE UNITED STATES OF AMERICA

ONE

THE SPIRES were not his own. The colors were not his own. He had a moment of shattering, blinding terror—and then calmness. He took a long breath of cold night air and began the job of working out his bearings.

He seemed to be on some kind of hillside, overgrown with brambles and vines. He was alive—and he still had his gray metal case. Experimentally, he tore the vines away and inched cautiously forward. Stars glittered above. Thank God for that. Familiar stars . . .

Not familiar.

He closed his eyes and hung on until his senses came trickling back. Then he pushed painfully down the side of the hill and toward the illuminated spires that lay perhaps a mile ahead, his case clutched in his hand.

Where was he? And why was he here? Had somebody *brought* him here, dumped him off at this spot for a reason?

The colors of the spires shifted and he began to work out, in a vague fashion, the equation of their pattern. By the time he was halfway he had it down fairly well. For some reason it made him feel better. Here was something he could predict. Get hold of. Above the spires, ships swirled and darted, swarms of them, catching the shifting lights. How beautiful it was.

This scene wasn't his, but it looked nice. And that was something. So this hadn't changed. Reason, beauty, cold winter air late at night. He quickened his

1

pace, stumbled, and then, pushing through trees, came out onto the smooth pavement of a highway.

He hurried.

As he hurried he let his thoughts wander around aimlessly. Bringing back the last fragments of sound and being, the final bits of a world abruptly gone. Wondering, in a detached, objective way, exactly what had happened.

Jim Parsons was on his way to work. It was a bright sunny morning. He had paused a moment to wave to his wife before getting into his car.

"Anything you want from town?" he called.

Mary stood on the front porch, hands in the pockets of her apron. "Nothing I can think of, darling. I'll vid you at the Institute if I remember anything."

In the warm sunlight Mary's hair shone a luminous auburn, a flashing cloud of flame which, this week was the new fashion among the wives. She stood small and slender in her green slacks and close-fitting foilite sweater. He waved to her, grabbed one final vision of his pretty wife, their one-story stucco house, the garden, the flagstone path, the California hills rising up in the distance, and then hopped into the car.

He spun off down the road, allowing the car to operate on the San Francisco guide-beam north. It was safer that way, especially on U.S. 101. And a lot quicker. He didn't mind having his car operated from a hundred miles off. All the other cars racing along the sixteen-lane highway were guide-operated, too, those going his way and those heading in the opposite direction, on the analog south highway to Los Angeles. It made accidents almost impossible, and meant he could enjoy the educational notices which various universities traditionally posted along the route. And, behind the notices, the countryside.

The countryside was fresh and well cared for. Attractive, since President Cantelli had nationalized the soap, tire, and hotel industries. No more ads to ruin the hills and valleys. Wouldn't be long before all industries were in the hands of the ten-man Economics Planning Board, operating under the Westinghouse research schools. Of course, when it came to doctors, that was another thing.

He tapped his instrument case on the seat beside him. Industry was one thing; the professional classes another. Nobody was going to nationalize the doctors, lawyers, painters, musicians. During the last decades the technocratic and professional classes had gradually gained control of society. By 1998, instead of business-men and politicians it was scientists rationally trained to—

Something picked up the car and hurled it from the road.

Parsons screamed as the car spun dizzily onto the shoulder and careened into the brush and educational signs. *The guide has failed.* That was his last thought. *Interference.* Trees, rocks, came looming up, bursting in on him. A shrieking crash of plastic and metal fused together, and his own voice, a chaotic clatter of sound and movement. And then the sickening impact that crumpled up the car like a plasti-carton. All the safety devices within the car—he dimly felt them scrambling into a belated action. Cushioning him, surrounding him, the odor of antifire spray . . .

He was thrown clear, into a rolling void of gray. He remembered spinning slowly, coming to earth like a weightless, drifting particle. Everything was slowed down, a tape track brought almost to a halt. He felt no pain. Nothing at all. An enormous formless mist seemed all around him.

A radiant field. A beam of some kind. The power which had interfered with the guide. He realized that— his last conscious thought. Then darkness descended over him.

He was still gripping his gray instrument case.

Ahead the highway broadened.

Lights flickered around him, geared to his presence. An advancing umbrella of yellow and green dots that showed him the way. The road entered and mixed with an intricate web of other roads, branches that faded into the darkness. He could only guess their directions.

At the hub of complex he halted and examined a sign which immediately came alive, apparently for his benefit. He read the unfamiliar words aloud:

"DIR 30c N; ATR 46c N; BAR 100c S; CRP 205s S; EGL 67cN."

N and *S* no doubt were north and south. But the rest meant nothing. The C was a unit of measurement. That had changed; the mile was no longer used. The magnetic pole was still used as a reference point, but that did not cheer him much.

Vehicles of some sort were moving along the roads that lifted above and beyond him. Drops of light. Similar to the spires of the city itself, they shifted hues as they altered space relationship with him.

Finally, he gave up on the sign. It told him only what he knew already, nothing more. He had gone ahead. A considerable jump. The language, the mensural system, the whole appearance of society had changed.

He hoisted himself from the lowest road up the steps of a hand-ramp to the next level. Quickly, he swung up to a third and then a fourth. Now he could see the city with ease.

It was really something. Big and beautiful. Without the constellation of industrial outfits ringing it, the chimneys and stacks that had made even San Francisco ugly. It took his breath away. Standing on the ramp in the cold night darkness, the wind rustling around him, the stars overhead, the moving drops of color that were the shifting vehicles, Parsons was overcome with emotion. The sight of the city made his heart ache. He began to walk again, buoyed up with vigor. His spirits were rising. What would he find? What kind of world? Whatever it was, he'd be able to function. The thought drummed triumphantly in his brain: *I'm a doctor. A heck of a good doctor. Now, if it were anybody else . . .*

A doctor would always be needed. He could master the language—an area in which he had always shown skill—and the social customs. Find a place for himself, survive while he discovered how he had gotten here. Eventually get back to his wife, of course. Yes, he thought, Mary would love this. Possibly reutilize the forces that had brought him here; relocate his family in this city. . .

Parsons gripped his gray metal case and hurried. And while he was hurrying breathlessly down the incline of the road, a silent drop of color detached itself from the ribbon beneath him, rose, and headed straight for him. Without hesitation, it aimed itself in his direction. He had time only to freeze; the color *whooshed* toward him—and he realized that it did not intend to miss.

"Stop!" he shouted. His arms came up reflexively; he was waving frantically at the burgeoning color, the thing so close now that it filled his eyes and blinded him.

It passed him, and as the hot wind blew around him, he made out a face which peered at him. Peered in mixed emotions. Amusement—and astonishment!

Parsons had an intuition. Difficult to believe, but he had seen it himself. The driver of the vehicle had been surprised at his reaction to being run down and killed.

Now the vehicle returned, more slowly this time, with the driver hanging his head out to stare at Parsons. The vehicle coasted to a stop beside him, its engine murmuring faintly.

"Hin?" the driver said.

Foolishly, Parsons thought, *But I didn't even have my thumb out.* Aloud he said, "Why, you tried to run me down." His voice shook.

The driver frowned. In the shifting colors his face seemed first dark blue, then orange; the lights made Parsons shut his eyes. The man behind the wheel was astonishingly young. A youth, hardly more than a boy. The whole thing was dreamlike, this boy who had never seen him before trying to run him down, then calmly offering him a ride.

The door of the vehicle slid back. *"Hin,"* the boy repeated, not in a commanding voice but with politeness.

At last, almost as a reflex, Parsons got shakily in. The door slammed shut and the car leaped forward. Parsons was crushed back against the seat by the velocity.

Beside him, the boy said something that Parsons

could not understand. His tone suggested that he was still amazed, still puzzled, and wanted to apologize. And the boy continued to glance at Parsons.

It was no game, Parsons realized. This boy really meant to run me down, to kill me. If I hadn't waved my arms—

And as soon as I waved my arms the boy stopped. *The boy thought I wanted to be run down!*

TWO

BESIDE HIM, the boy drove with easy confidence. Now the car had turned toward the city; the boy leaned back and released the controls. His curiosity about Parsons clearly was growing stronger. Turning his seat so that he faced Parsons, he studied him. Reaching up, he snapped on an interior light that made both of them more visible.

And, in the light, Parsons got his first real look at the boy. And what he saw jarred him.

Dark hair, shiny and long. Coffee-colored skin. Flat, wide cheek bones. Almond eyes that glinted liquid in the reflected light. A prominent nose. Roman?

No, Parsons thought. Almost Hittite. And his black hair . . .

The man was certainly multiracial. The cheek bones suggested Mongolian. The eyes were Mediterranian. The hair possibly Negroid. The skin color, perhaps, had an underglint of reddish brown. Polynesian?

On the boy's shirt—he wore a dark red, two-piece robe, and slippers—an embroidered herald caught Parson's attention. A stylized eagle.

Eagle. *Egl.* And the others. *Dir* was deer. *Bar* was bear. The rest he couldn't guess. What did this animal nomenclature mean? He started to speak, but the youth cut him off.

"Whur venis a tardus?" he demanded in his not entirely grown-up voice.

Parsons was floored. The language, although unfamiliar, was not alien. It had a baffingly natural ring; something almost understood, but not quite.

"What?" he asked.

The youth qualified his question. *"Ye kleidis novae en sagis novate. Whur iccidi hist?"*

Now he began to get the drift. Like the boy's racial cast, the language was a polyglot. Evidently based on Latin, and possibly an artificial language, a lingua franca; made up of the most familiar bits possible. Pondering the words, Parsons came to the conclusion that the boy wanted to know why he was out so late and why he dressed so strangely. And why he spoke as he did. But at the moment he did not feel inclined to give answers; he had questions of his own.

"I want to know," he said slowly and carefully, "why you tried to run me down."

Blinking, the boy said haltingly, *"Whur ik . . ."* His voice trailed off. Obviously, he did not understand Parson's words.

Or was it that the words were understood, but the question was incomprehensible? With a further chill, Parsons thought, maybe it's supposed to be self-evident. Taken for granted. Of course he tried to kill me. Doesn't everybody?

Feeling a profound resurgence of alarm, he settled down to get at the language barrier. I'm going to have to make myself understood, he realized. And right away.

To the boy, he said, "Keep talking."

"Sag?" the boy repeated. *"Ik sag yer, ye meinst?"*

Parsons nodded. "That's right," he said. Ahead of them, the city came closer and closer. "You've got it." We're making progress, he thought grimly. And he stiffened himself to listen as carefully as possible as the boy, haltingly, prattled on. We're making progress, but I wonder if there's going to be enough time.

A broad span carried the car over a moat which surrounded the city, a purely ornamental moat, from the brief glimpse that Parsons caught of it. More and more cars became visible, moving quite slowly, and now people on foot. He made out the sight of crowds, great masses moving along ramps, entering and leaving the spires, pushing along sidewalks. All the people that he saw seemed young. Like the boy beside him. And they, too, had the dark skin, the flat cheek bones, and the robes. He saw a variety of emblems. Animal, fish, and bird heralds.

Why? Society organized by totem tribes? Or different races? Or was some festival in progress? But they were physically alike, and that made him discard the theory that each emblem represented a different race. An arbitrary division of the population?

Games?

All wore their hair long, braided, and tied in back, both men and women. The men were considerably larger than the women. They had stern noses and chins. The women hurried along, laughing and chattering, bright-eyed, lips luminous and striking, unusually full. But so young—almost children. Merry, laughing boys and girls. At an intersection a hanging light gave off the first full-spectrum white that he had seen in this world, so far; in its stark glare he saw that the lips of both men and women had a black color, not red at all. And it's not the light, he decided. Although it could be a dye. Mary used to show up with those fashionable hair dyes . . .

In this first genuinely revealing light, the boy beside him was staring at him with a new expression. He had halted the car.

"Agh," the boy gasped. And on his face the expression became obvious. Drawing back, he shrank against the far door of the car. "*Ye—*" He stammered for words, and at last burst out chokingly, and so loudly that several passers-by glanced up, "*Ye bist sick!*"

That word was a remnant of Parsons' language: it could not be mistaken. The tone itself, and the boy's expression, removed any doubt.

"Why sick?" Parsons answered, nettled and defensive. "I can tell you for a certainty—"

Interrupting him, the boy spat out a series of rapid-fire accusations. Some of the words—enough—were understandable. Finally he was beginning to catch the pattern of speech. And this was what he got: realization that now, having seen him clearly for the first time, the boy was overcome with aversion and disgust. The accusations poured out at Parsons in an almost hysterical tirade, while he sat helpless. And outside the car, a group of people had gathered to listen.

The door on Parsons' side of the car slid open; the boy had jabbed at a button on the control panel. I'm being ejected, Parsons realized. Protestingly, he tried to break into the tirade once more.

"Look here," he began. At that point he broke off. Standing on the pavement outside the car, the people who had caught sight of him had the same expression on their faces. The same horror and dismay. The same disgust as the boy. The people murmured, and he saw a woman raise her hand and indicate something to those behind who couldn't quite see. The woman indicated her own face.

My white skin! Parsons realized.

"Are you going to drop me out there?" he said to the boy, and indicated the murmuring crowd.

The boy hesitated. Even if he did not quite grasp Parsons' words he could follow his meaning. There was hostility in the crowd as it jostled for a better look at Parsons, and the boy saw that; both he and Parsons heard the angry tones and saw the movement of more definite purpose.

With a whirr, the door beside Parsons slid shut. It locked, with him still inside the car. Bending forward, the boy caught hold of the car's controls; the car at once moved rapidly forward.

"Thanks," Parsons said.

Without answering him, or even paying any attention to him, the boy made the car pick up speed. Now they had reached an ascending ramp; the car shot up it and leveled off at the top. Glancing out, the boy slowed the car almost to a halt. To their left Parsons made out a less brightly lighted avenue. The car moved in that direction and came to rest in half-shadows. The structures here seemed poorer, less ornate. And no people were in sight.

Again the door slid open.

Parsons said, "I appreciate it." Shakily, he stepped out.

The boy shut the door, and then the car shot off and out of sight. Parsons found himself standing alone, still trying to frame a statement or ask some question—he did not know which. Suddenly the car reappeared; without slowing it hurtled by him, once again breathing its hot exhaust breath at him, sending him spinning back to escape its gleaming lights. From the car something sailed out and crashed at Parsons' feet.

His instrument case. He had left it in the car.

Seated in the shadows, he opened his instrument case and inspected the contents. Nothing appeared broken or damaged. Thank God for that.

Mercifully, the boy had let him off in a warehouse district. The buildings had a massive quality, with enormous double doors clearly not intended for human traffic but for some kind of oversized vehicles. And, on the pavement around him, he saw the dim outline of refuse.

He picked up a piece of written material. A political pamphlet, evidently. Denouncing someone or some party. He recognized words here and there—the syntax seemed easy enough; the language was inflected, along the lines of Spanish or Italian, not distributive, but with occasional English words. Seeing it written made the problem of understanding it much easier for him. He recalled the medical texts in Russian and Chinese that had been required reading, the twice-monthly journal with abstracts in six languages. Part of being a medical man. At the University of La Jolla he had had to read not only German, Russian, Chinese, but also French— a language of no real current importance, but forced on them by tradition. And his wife, as a cultural asset, had been learning classic Greek.

Anyhow, he realized, that's all solved now. They have their one synthetic language. And this is it.

What I need is a place to hide, he decided. While I

orient myself—a breathing-spell, where I'm less vulnerable. The buildings, dark and silent around him, appeared deserted. At the end of the street, a variety of lights and the tiny, distant shapes of people indicated a commercial section, open in the night to do business.

A dim street light lit the way ahead of him as he walked cautiously among the discarded cartons heaped by a loading platform. Now he stumbled over a series of waste-cans, from which a muted churning became audible. The overflowing waste began to stir, and he discovered that by knocking against the cans he had started the mechanism back into operation. No doubt it was supposed to be automatic, consuming trash as fast as it was put in, but it hadn't been kept in good repair.

A flight of cement steps led down to a doorway. He descended and tried the rusty handle of the door. Locked, of course. A storage area, probably.

Kneeling down in the semidarkness he opened his instrument case and got out the surgical packet. Its power supply was self-contained, and he clicked it on. The basic tools lit up; for emergency operations they cast enough light to work by. Expertly, he fitted a cutting blade into the drive-gear socket and cinched it up. Whining faintly, the blade cut into the lock of the door. He stood close to it, muffling the sound.

The blade crunched loose; the lock had been cut away from the door. Hastily, he disassembled the surgical tools, stuffed them back into the instrument case. With both hands he gently tugged at the door.

The door opened, squeaking on its hinges.

Now, he thought. A place to hide. In his case he had a number of dermal preparations, for use in treating burns. Already he had selected in his mind the combination of aseptic sprays that would yield a darker color; he could lower his skin hue to one indistinguishable from that of . . .

In sudden bright light he stood blinking. Not a deserted storeroom at all. Warm air greeted him, smells of food. A man stood with a decanter in his hand, stopped in the act of pouring a woman's drink.

Seven or eight people faced him. Some sitting in

chairs, a couple standing. They regarded him placidly, without surprise. They had obviously been aware of him while he cut away the lock; they had heard him outside, working.

The man resumed pouring the woman's drink. Now a low-pitched murmur of talk picked up. His presence—manner of entry—did not seem to perturb these people at all.

A woman, seated near him, was saying something to him. The musical flow of words repeated themselves several times, but he could not catch the meaning. The woman smiled up at him, without rancor, again speaking, but now more slowly. He caught one word, then another. She was telling him firmly but politely that it was up to him to replace the door lock.

". . . and please shut it." she concluded. "The door."

Foolishly, he reached behind him and pulled the door shut.

A dapper-looking youth, leaning toward him, said, "We know who you are." At least, so Parsons interpreted his statement.

"Yes," another man said. Several of them nodded.

The woman near the door said, "You're the—" And a word followed that he could make no sense of. It had a totally artificial ring, jargon rather than language.

"That's right," another echoed. "That's what you are."

"But we don't care," a boy said.

They all agreed to that.

"Because," the boy continued, his white teeth sparkling, "we're not here."

A chorus of agreement, "No, not here at *all*!"

"This is a delusion," a slender woman said.

"Delusion," two men repeated.

Parsons said unsteadily, "Who am I, did you say?"

"So we're not afraid," one of them said, or at least so he understood that person to say.

"Afraid?" Parsons said. That caught his attention at once.

"You came to get us," a girl said.

"Yes," they all agreed, with evident delight, their heads nodding up and down. "But you can't."

He thought, *They think I'm somebody else.*

"Touch me," the woman by the door said. She set down her drink and rose from her chair. "I'm not actually here."

"None of us are," several people agreed. "Touch her. Go on."

Unable to move, Parsons stood where he was. *I don't get it*, he thought. *I just don't.*

"All right," the woman said. "I'll touch you. My hand will pass right through yours."

"Like air," a man said happily.

The woman reached out her slim, dark fingers, closer and closer to his arm. Smiling, her eyes alive with delight, she put her fingers on his arm.

Her fingers did not pass through. At once, her mouth fell open with shock. "Oh," she whispered.

The room became silent. They all stared at him.

Finally one of the men said faintly, "He's genuinely found us."

"He really is here," a woman murmured, her eyes wild with fear. "Here where we are. In the basement."

They gazed at Parsons numbly. He could do nothing but gaze back.

THREE

AFTER a terrible silence, one of the women sank down in a chair and said, "We thought you were up on Fingal Street. We have a projection on Fingal Street."

"How did you find us?" a man said. Their rather adolescent voices mingled in a chorus.

Of the welter of talk he could make out a reasonable portion. A meeting. Secret, down here in the warehouse district. So sure of their seclusion that his coming hadn't registered.

Shupo. That had been the word for him.

With great care, Parsons said. "I'm not *shupo*." Whatever that was.

At once, they perked up. All eyes again fixed on him, the black, large, youthful eyes.

A man said, with bitterness. "Who else drills through doors?"

"Not only does he drill," a girl said. "but he's enmask."

They nodded. Their anxiety had become tinged with resentment.

"That incredible white mask," a girl said.

"We had masks," a man said. "The last time."

"Oftentimes," another said, "we wear masks when we're out."

He had, apparently, stumbled onto a marginal, covert group that operated outside the law. Conspiring, possibly political . . . in danger. Certainly in no position to menace him. Good luck for me, he decided.

"Let's see your real face," a man said. Now they all clamored, with mounting indignation.

"This is my real face," he said.

"All *white* like that?"

"And listen to him talk," another said. "Speech impediment."

"Partly deaf, too," another said, a girl. "In that he doesn't get half of what's said."

"A real *quivak*," a boy said scathingly.

A small, sharp-faced youth swaggered up to Parsons. With contempt, in a drawling, insinuating voice, he said close to Parsons' face, "Let's get it over with." He held up his right thumb.

"Cut it off," a girl said, her eyes flashing. She also held out her right thumb. "Go ahead. Cut it off right now!"

So, Parsons thought. Political criminals are maimed in this society. Ancient punishment. He felt deep revulsion. Barbaric . . . and these animal totems. Reversion to tribes.

And on the highway, the boy who thought I wanted to be killed. Who tried to ride me down and was perplexed when I tried to escape.

He thought, And the city looked so beautiful to me.

Off in the corner stood a man who had said nothing, who sipped his drink and watched. His dark, heavy features had an ironic expression; of them all, he seemed the only one who had control of his emotions. Now he moved toward Parsons and for the first time spoke up.

"You expected to find nobody here," he said. "You thought this was an empty warehouse."

Parsons nodded.

"The only complexion of your type," the man continued, "in my experience, is the result of a highly contagious plague. But you seem healthy. I notice also that you have unpigmented eyes."

"Blue," a girl corrected.

"That is unpigmented," the heavy-set man continued. "What interests me most is your clothing. I'd guess 1910."

With care, Parsons said, "More like 2010."

The man smiled slightly. "Not far off, though."

"What's this, then?" Parsons asked.

The black eyes flickered. "Ah," he said. Turning to the group he said. "Well, *amici*, this is less threatening than you imagine. We have here another botch tempuswise. I suggest we get the door relocked, and then sit down and cool." To Parsons, he said, "This is 2405. You're the first person that I know of. Up to now it's been *things*. Displacements. Said to be natural but freak. Frogs fall in the street, an extinct species. That tips off our scientific men. Stones. Debris. Bric-a-brac. You see?"

"Yes," Parsons said hesitantly.

The man shrugged. "But who can tell why." Again he smiled at Parsons. "Name's Wade," he said. "Yours?"

"Parsons."

"Hail," Wade said, lifting his open palm. "Or what is it? Noses? No matter. You care to join our party? Not frolic, but the other usage."

"Political," Parsons said.

"Yes, to change—not understand—society. I lead, here. The—what is your old word? Sill? Sold?"

"Cell," Parsons said.

"Quite right," Wade said. "As in bees, honey. Care to hear our program? Couldn't possibly mean anything to you. I suggest you exit. There is some danger to us."

Parsons said, "I've had trouble outside. For me there's danger out there, too." He indicated his face. "At least give me time to work on my color."

"Caucasic," Wade said, tasting the word as he said it, scowling.

"Give me half an hour," Parsons said tightly.

Wade made a gesture of largess. "Be our guest." He eyed Parsons. "We—they, if you will—have rigid standards. Maybe we can fit in. Unfortunately, no middle ground. Law of the excluded middle, sort of."

"In other words," Parsons said, feeling his tension and aversion rise, "it's like all primitive societies. The stranger isn't considered human. Killed on sight, is he? Anything unfamiliar." His hands were shaking; getting out a cigarette he lit it, trying to steady himself. "Your totem-device," he said, gesturing at Wade. "The eagle. You exhalt eagle qualities? Ruthlessness and quickness?"

"Not exactly," Wade said. "All tribes are unified, with common world view. We know nothing about eagles. Our tribal names came out of the Age of Darkness that followed the H-War."

Kneeling down, Parsons opened his instrument case. As quickly as possible he laid out his dermal sprays. Wade and the others watched for a few moments, and then seemed to lose interest. Their talk resumed. He thought, Short span of attention. Like children.

Not even like. Are. As yet he hadn't seen anyone over twenty or so. Wade had the most mature manner, the grave, educated pomposity of a left-wing college sophomore. Of course, he hadn't as yet seen a real sample. This group, the boy on the highway . . .

The door opened suddenly. A woman entered. At sight of Parsons she stopped. "Oh," she gasped. Her dark eyes widened with astonishment. "Who. . . ?"

Wade greeted her. "Icara. This is not illness. This is one of those frogs. Displacement named Parsons." To Parsons he said, "She is—my doxy? Bawd? Great and good friend? Puella."

The woman nodded nervously. She set down an armload of packages, which the other persons immediately gathered up. "Why is your skin chalk-colored?" she asked, bending down beside him, slender, breathing a little rapidly, her black lips twisting with concern.

"In my times," he said with difficulty, "we were divided into white, yellow, brown, black races. All varieties of sub-races within the species. It's obvious there was a fusion sometime later on."

Icara's finely-shaped nose wrinkled. "Separate? How awful. And your language is foul. Full of lapses. Why is the door hanging open?"

"He cut the lock," Wade sighed.

"Then he should fix it," the woman said with no

hesitation. Still bending down beside him, watching him work, she said. "What's that gray box? Why are you opening those tubes? Are you going to travel back in time? Can we watch?"

"He's spraying himself," Wade said. "Darker."

Her shining dark hair came closer to him as she leaned forward and delicately sniffed. In a low voice she said to him, "Also, you should do something about your smell."

"What?" he said, jolted on several levels.

Studying him, she said, "You smell bad. Like mold."

The others, overhearing, came over to see and then give their opinions. "More like vegetables," one man said. "Maybe it's his clothes. Vegetable fiber, possibly."

Icara said, "We bathe."

"So do we," Parsons said, with anger.

"Every day?" She drew back. "I believe it's your clothes, not you." She eyed him as he sprayed on his skin-coloring. "That's a good deal better. God, you looked like a grub. Not—"

"Not human," Parsons finished ironically.

Standing up, Icara said to Wade, "I don't see—I mean, it's going to be such a problem. The Soul Cube will be thrown off. And how can he possibly be fitted with the Fountain? He's so very different, and anyhow we don't have time for this; we have to get on with the meeting. And there our door is, hanging open."

"Is that bad?" Parsons demanded.

"The door?" she said.

"To be different."

"Why, of course it's bad. If you're different then you don't belong. But you can learn. Wade will give you the right clothing. You can learn to speak correctly. And look—those dyes of yours are working quite well." She smiled at him hopefully.

"Real problem," Wade said, "is orientation. He can't possibly learn. Basic concepts lacking; we got as babies." Raising an eyebrow he said to Parsons. "How old are you?"

"Thirty-two," Parsons said. He had almost finished

spraying his face, neck, hands and arms; now he had begun removing his shirt.

Wade and Icara exchanged glanced. "Oh, dear," Icara said. "You mean it? Thirty-two?" Evidently to change the subject she said. "What is that clever little gray box, and those objects in it?"

"My instruments," Parsons said, his shirt off now.

"And what about the Lists?" Wade said, half to himself. "The government won't like it." He shook his head. "He can't be fitted into any of the tribes. He'll throw the count off."

Parsons shoved the open instrument case toward Wade. "Look," he said harshly. "I don't give a damn about your tribes. You see these? They're the finest surgical tools developed in twenty-six centuries. I don't know how good or how extensive your own medical work is, but I can hold my own in any culture, past or present. With my kind of knowledge and skill, I can be of value anywhere, I know that, if nothing else. My medical knowledge will always find me a place!"

Icara and Wade looked blank. "Medical knowledge?" Icara faltered. "What's that?"

Parsons, appalled, said, "I'm a physician."

"You're a —" Icara searched for the word. "What was it I read in the history tape? Alchemist? No, that's earlier. Sorcerer? Is a physician a sorcerer? Does he predict events by examining the motion of the stars, and consulting with spirits and so on?"

"How dull," Wade murmured. "There are no spirits."

Now Parsons had sprayed his chest, shoulders and back; as rapidly as possible he rebuttoned his shirt, hoping that the film had dried. He put on his coat, tossed his instruments back in the case, and started toward the half-open door.

Wade said, "*Salvay, amicus.*" He sounded gloomy.

Pausing at the door, Parsons turned to speak, but the door, on its own, whipped away from him. Half falling, he lurched, caught himself—and looked down into a grinning, sardonic little face that peered up at him gleefully. A child, he thought. A ghastly caricature of a child, and more of them, all wearing the same dainty green cap . . . costumes in a grammar school play. Pointing a metal tube at him, the first child shrilled:

"*Shupo!*"

He managed to kick the first *shupo*; his toe caught it and lifted it up. It still shrilled, even as it crashed into the cement wall that rose from the entranceway. But while he kicked it, the others swarmed past him, between his legs, up him and over him, their nails tearing at him, as they scrabbled on by, into the meeting room.

His arms in front of his face, he plowed his way up the steps, to the street.

Below him, the *shupos* clustered at the door like venomous green wasps. He could not make out what was happening inside; he saw only their backs, and he could hear nothing but their shouts. They had the political people trapped. They did not care about him, or, if they did, they had not had time to snare him. Now, he saw their vehicles. Several had been placed to block the street. Possibly the unlocked, half-open door had let out light, which had attracted a routine patrol. Or they had followed the woman, Icara. He did not know. Perhaps they had even followed him, all the way from the start.

They lose their thumbs, do they? he wondered. And voluntarily? It did not sound as if the group had decided to submit; the uproar was growing. If I brought the *shupos* here, he thought, I'm responsible; I can't run off. Hesitantly, he started back.

From the undulating mass in the shadows at the base of the stairs, two full-grown shapes split apart and emerged. A man and a woman, fighting their way up, gasping. He saw, with horror, trails of blood dripping and glistening on their faces. Not thumbs, he thought. They're fighting, and it doesn't end. That's the sacrifice, but if they won't make it, then—their lives?

The man, Wade, called hoarsely up to him, "Parsons!" His arms lifted; he tried to propel the girl up the steps. *Shupos* clung to every part of him. "Please!" he called, his eyes blind, agonized.

Parsons came back. Dropping down the stairwell, both feet stamping, he caught hold of the girl.

Sinking back, Wade again merged, pulled back by the *shupos*, into the darkness and noise; the green shapes gleamed, shrieking in triumph. Blood, Parsons thought. They're getting blood. Holding the girl against him he struggled up the stairs, gasping; he reached the street, staggered. Blood ran down his wrists, from the girl's body. Warm, boneless, she slipped closer to him as he walked. Her head lolled. Her untied hair, shimmering spread out. Icara. Not surprising, he thought in a dulled fashion. Love before politics.

Here, in the darkness of the street, he wandered along, panting for breath, his clothing torn, carrying Wade's doxy, or girl, or whatever. Do they have last names? he asked himself.

The noise of the fracas had attracted passers-by; they flocked, calling excitedly. Several glanced at Parsons as he carried the unconscious girl. Dead? No. He could feel her heart beating. The passers-by hurried on in the opposite direction, to the scene of the fighting.

Worn out, he halted to gather up the girl and hoist her up onto his shoulder. Her face brushed his, the excellent smooth skin. Lips, he thought, warm and moist . . . what a pretty woman. Twenty or so.

Turning the corner he continued on, almost unable to proceed. His lungs hurt and he had trouble seeing. Now he had come out onto a brightly lighted street. He saw many people, a glimpse of stores, signs, parked vehicles. Activity, and the pleasant background of leisure. From the doorway of a store—a dress shop, by the looks of the window display—music swirled, and he recognized it: the Beethoven *Archduke Trio*. Bizarre, he thought.

Ahead, a hotel. At least, a great many-storied building, with trees, wrought-iron railing, vehicles in rows before it. Reaching the steps, he ascended into a lobby in which people moved about. What he meant to do he did not know, for all at once, against him, the girl's heartbeat fluttered, became irregular.

He had his instrument case, didn't he? Yes, he had

managed to hold onto it. Setting the girl down, he opened the case.

People milled around him. "Get the hotel euthanor!"

"Her own. She has her own euthanor."

Parsons said, "No time." And he began to work.

FOUR

CLOSE BY his ear, a polite but authoritative voice said, "Do you need assistance?"

Parsons said, "No. Except—" He glanced up from his work for a moment. Into the girl's chest he had plugged a Dixon pump; it had taken over temporarily the job of her uneven heart.

Beside him stood a man wearing a nondescript white robe, without emblem. Like the others, he was in his twenties. But his voice and manner were not the same, and in his hand he held a flat, black-bordered card.

"Keep the people back," Parsons said, and resumed work. The throb of the robot pump gave him confidence; it had been inserted very well, and the load had left the girl's circulatory system.

Over her lacerated right shoulder he sprayed art-derm; it sealed off the open wound, halted bleeding and prohibited infection. The most serious damage was to her windpipe. He turned the little art-derm nozzle on an exposed section of rib, wondering what the *shupos* had that worked so well. It had carved her open expertly, whatever it was. Now he turned his attention to her windpipe.

Beside him the polite official put away his identification card and said, "Are you certain you know what you're doing?" He had, at least, cleared away the people. Evidently his rank affected them; the lobby had become empty. "Maybe we should call the building euthanor."

The hell with him, Parsons thought. "I'm doing fine," he said aloud. His fingers flew. Twisting, cutting, spraying, breaking open plastic tubes of tissue graft, fitting them into place.

"Yes," the official said. "I can see. You're an expert. By the way, my name's Al Stenog."

At least, Parsons thought, a man with a last name.

"This furrow," Parsons said, tracing the line that crossed the girl's stomach. He had coated it with air-proof plastic. "It looks bad, but it's merely into the fatty wall, not the abdominal cavity." He showed Stenog the damaged windpipe. "That's the worst."

"I think I see the building euthanor," Stenog said in an affable voice. "Yes, somebody must have called him. Do you want him to assist you?"

"No," Parsons said.

"It's your decision," Stenog said. "I won't interfere." He was staring at Parsons with curiosity.

My speech, Parsons thought. But he could not worry about that, now. At least he had altered the color of his skin. My eyes! he realized suddenly. As Wade said: unpigmented.

I have to save this girl's life, he decided. That's first.

With the official watching over his shoulder, he continued his job of healing the girl.

"I failed to catch your name," Stenog said unobtrusively.

"Parsons," he answered.

"That's an odd name," Stenog said. "What does it mean?"

"Nothing," Parsons said.

"Oh?" Stenog murmured. He was silent, then, for a time, as Parsons worked. "Interesting," he said at last.

A second shape appeared beside Stenog. Parsons, taking a moment to glance up, saw a carefully groomed, handsome man with something under his arm, a kit of some kind. The euthanor.

"It's all over," Parsons said. "I took care of her."

"I'm a little late," the euthanor admitted. "I was out of the building." His eyes strayed, as he took in the sight of the girl. "Did this occur here? In the hotel?"

Stenog said, "No, Parsons brought her in from the street." To Parsons he said in his smooth voice, "A vehicle accident? Or an assault? You neglected to say."

Parsons simply didn't answer; he concentrated on the final portion of the job.

The girl would live. In another half minute her life would have ebbed out of her throat and chest, and then nothing would have saved her. His skill, his knowledge, had saved her life, and these two men—evidently respected individuals in this society—were witnesses to it.

"I can't follow your work," the euthanor admitted. "I've never seen anything like it. Who are you? Where did you come from? How did you learn techniques like that?" To Stenog he said, "I'm completely baffled. I don't recognize any of his accessories."

"Perhaps Parsons will tell us," Stenog said softly. "Of course, this is hardly the time. A little later, no doubt."

"Does it matter," Parsons said, "where I come from, or who I am?"

Stenog said, "I've been informed that there's police action going on around the corner. This girl might be from that event, possibly. You were passing nearby, found the girl injured on the street, brought her . . ."

His voice trailed off questioningly, but Parsons said nothing.

Now Icara was beginning to regain consciousness. She gave a faint cry and moved her arms.

There was a moment of stunned silence. "What does this mean?" the euthanor demanded.

"I've been successful," Parsons said irritably. "Better get her into a bed. There's damage that'll have to heal over a period of weeks." What did they expect, a miracle? "But there's no longer any danger."

"No longer any danger?" Stenog repeated.

"That's right," Parsons said. What was the matter with them? "She'll recover. Understand?"

In a slow, cautious voice, Stenog said, "Then in what sense have you been successful?"

Parsons stared at him, and Stenog stared back with a faintly contemptuous expression.

Examining the girl, the euthanor began to tremble. "I understand," he said in a choked voice. "You pervert! You maniac!"

As if he were enjoying the situation, Stenog said in a pleasant, light voice, "Parsons, you've blatantly healed the girl. Isn't that a fact? These are therapeutic devices you have here. I'm amazed." He seemed almost to laugh. "Well, of course you're under arrest. You realize that." With firmness, he moved the furious-faced euthanor back. "I'll handle this," he said. "This is my business, not yours. You can go. If you're needed as a witness, my office will get in touch with you."

As the euthanor reluctantly left, Parsons found himself facing Stenog alone. Leisurely, Stenog brought forth what looked to Parsons like an eggbeater. Touching a raised spot on its handle, Stenog sent the blades into spinning motion; the blades disappeared and from it came a high-pitched whine. Obviously, it was a weapon.

"You're under arrest," Stenog said. "For a major crime against the United Tribes. The Folk." The words had a formal sound, but not the man's tone; he spoke them as if they had no importance to him; it was a mere ritual. "Follow me, if you will."

Parsons said, "You're serious?"

The younger man raised a dark eyebrow. He motioned with the eggbeater. He *was* serious. "You're lucky," he said to Parsons, as they moved toward the entrance to the hotel. "If you had healed her there, with those tribe people . . ." Again he eyed Parsons with curiosity. "They would have torn you apart. But of course you knew that."

This society is insane, Parsons thought. This man and this society together.

I am really afraid!

In the dimly lighted room the two shapes watched the

glowing procession of words avidly, leaning forward in their chairs, powerful bodies taut.

"Too late!" the strong-faced man cursed bitterly. "Everything was out of phase. No accurate junction with the dredge. And now he's trapped in an intertribal area." Pressing a control, he speeded up the flow of words. "And now, someone from the government."

"What's the matter with the emergency team?" the woman beside him whispered. "Why aren't they there? They could have got him on the street. The first flash was sent out as soon as—"

"It takes time." The strong-faced man paced restlessly back and forth, feet lost in the thick carpets that covered the floor. "If only we could have come out in the open."

"They won't get there soon enough." The seated woman struck out savagely, and the flow of illuminated words faded. "By the time they get there he'll be dead—or worse. So far we've completely failed, Helmar. It's gone wrong."

Noise. Lights and movement around him. For an instant he opened his eyes. A shattering blaze of white pooured remorselessly down on him from all sides; once more he shut his eyes. It hadn't changed.

"Your name again?" a voice said. "Name, please."

He did not answer.

"James Parsons," another voice said. A familiar voice. As he heard it he wondered dully whose voice it was. He could almost place it. Almost, but not quite.

"Old?"

"Thirty-two," the voice said, after a pause. And this time he recognized it; the voice was his, and he was answering their questions without volition. Off somewhere, machinery hummed.

"Born?" the voice asked.

Once more he struggled to open his eyes. His hand came up to shield his eyes from the glare, and he saw, for a moment, the blur of objects and people. A clerk, bored, empty-faced, seated at a recording machine, writing down the answers that were given. A bureaucrat. A functionary in a clean office. No force, no violence. The answers came, however. *Why do I tell them?*

"Chicago, Illinois," his voice, from some other point in the room, answered. "Cook County."

The clerk said presently, "What month, date?"

"October 16," his voice answered. "1980."

On the clerk's face the expression remained the same. "Brothers or sisters?"

"No." his voice said.

On and on the questions went. And he answered each one of them.

"All right, Mr. Parsons," the clerk said at last.

"Dr. Parsons," the voice—his voice—corrected, from a learned reflex.

The clerk paid no attention. "You're through," he said, removing a spool from the recording machine. "Will you go across the hall to Room 34, please?" With a nod of his chin he indicated the direction. "They'll take care of you there."

Stiffly, Parsons rose. A table, he discovered. He had been sitting on a table, and he had on only his shorts. Like a hospital—aseptic, white, professional looking. He began to walk. And, as he did so, he saw his white legs, unsprayed, a strange contrast to his dyed arms, chest, back, and neck. So they know, he thought. But he kept on walking. In him there was no desire either to comply or to resist; he simply walked from the interrogation room, down a well-lit hall, to Room 34.

The door opened as he approached. Now he found himself standing in what appeared to be a personal apartment. He saw, with amazement, a harpsichord. Cushions upon a window seat, a window that overlooked the city. Midday, by the looks of the sun. Books here and there, and, on the wall, a reproduction of a Picasso.

While he stood there, Stenog appeared, leafing through a clipboard of papers. Glancing at Parsons he said, "Even the deformed? The congenitally deformed? You healed *them* too?"

"Sure," Parsons said. Now, some sense of control

had begun to filter back into him. "I—" he began haltingly, but Stenog broke in.

"I have read about your period on the history tapes," Stenog said. "You're a *doctor*. Well, that term is clear. I understand the function you performed. But I can't grasp the ideology behind it. *Why?*" His face became animated with emotion. "That girl, Icara. She was dying, and yet you deliberately made skillful alterations to her system for the purpose of keeping her alive."

Parsons answered with an effort. "That's right."

Now he saw that several other persons had accompanied Stenog into the room. They hung back, out of the way, letting Stenog do the talking.

"In your culture this had a positive value?" Stenog said. "Such an act was officially sanctioned?"

A person in the background said, "Your profession was honored? A valued social role, with plaudits?"

Stenog said, "I find it impossible to believe a whole society could have been oriented around such behavior. Surely it was a splinter group that sanctioned you."

Parsons heard them, but their words made no sense. Everything was out of focus. Distorted. As if turned out by some warped mirror. "Healing was respected," he managed to say. "But you people seem to think it's somehow wrong."

A furious rustle leaped through the circle of listeners. "Wrong!" Stenog snapped. "It's madness! Don't you see what would happen if everybody were healed? All the sick and injured? The old?"

"No wonder his society collapsed," a harsh-eyed girl said. "It's amazing it stood so long. Based on such a perverted system of values."

"It demonstrates," Stenog said thoughtfully, "the almost infinite variety of cultural formations. That a whole society could exist oriented around such drives seems to us beyond belief. But from our historical reconstruction we know such a thing actually went on. This man here is not an escaped lunatic. In his own time he was a valued person. His profession had not only sanction—it gave him prestige."

The girl said, "Intellectually, I can accept it. But not emotionally."

A cunning expression appeared on Stenog's face. "Parsons, let me ask you this. I recall a pertinent fact. Your science was also devoted to keeping new life from appearing. You had contraceptives. Chemical and mechanical agents preventing zygote formation within the oviduct."

Parsons started to answer. "We—"

"*Rassmort!*" the girl snarled, pale with fury.

Parsons blinked. What did that mean? He couldn't convert it into his own semantic system.

"Do you remember the average age of your population?" Stenog asked.

"No," Parsons muttered. "About forty, I believe."

At that, the roomful of persons broke into jeers. "Forty!" Stenog said, with disgust. "*Our* agerage age is fifteen."

It meant nothing to Parsons. Except that, as he had already seen, there were few old people. "You consider that something to be proud of?" he said wonderingly.

A roar of indignation burst from the circle around him. "All right," Stenog said, gesturing. "I want you all to leave; you're making it impossible for me to perform my job."

They left reluctantly.

When the last had gone, Stenog walked to the window and stood for a moment.

"We had no idea," he said at last to Parsons, over his shoulder. "When I brought you in here, it was for a routine examination." He paused. "Why didn't you dye your body all over? Why just in parts?"

Parsons said, "No time."

"You've just been here briefly." Stenog glanced over the written material on his clipboard. "I see that you claim no knowledge of how you got from your time segment to ours. Interesting."

If it was all there, there was no point in him saying anything. He remained silent. Past Stenog he could see the city, and he began to take an interest in it. The spires . . .

"What bothers me," Stenog said, "is that we dropped experimentation with time travel something like eight years ago. The government, I mean. A principle was put forth, showing that time travel was a limited application of perpetual motion, and hence a contradiction of its own working laws. That is, if you wanted to invent a time machine, all you'd have to do was swear or prophesy that when you got it working, the first use you'd put it to would be to go back into time, to the point at which you got interested in the idea." He smiled. "And give your earlier self the functioning, finished piece of equipment. This has never happened; evidently there can be no time travel. By definition, time travel is a discovery that, if it could be made, *would already have been made*. Perhaps I oversimplified the proof, but substantially—"

Parsons interrupted. "That assumes that if the discovery had already been made, it would be publicly known. Recognized. But nobody saw me leave my own world." He gestured. "And do you think they realize now what's happened? All they know is that I disappeared, with no trace. Would they infer that I was carried into time?" He thought of his wife. "They don't know," he said. "There was no warning." Now he told Stenog the details; the younger man listened attentively.

"A force field," Stenog said presently. With a sudden shudder of anger he said, "We shouldn't have given up experimentation; we had a good deal of basic research done, hardware constructed." Now, he pondered. "That hardware—God knows what became of it. The research never was kept secret. Presumably the hardware was sold off; a lot of valuable components were involved. That was last year or so. We had it so clearly in mind that time travel would show up in some vast historic way, interfere with the collapse of the Greek City States, assist the success of Napoleon's European plan and thereby obviate the following wars. But you're implying a *secret*, limited time travel. For some personal reasons. Not official, not for social aims." His boyish face drew into a troubled scowl.

"If you recognize that I'm from another time," Parsons said, "from another culture, how can you convict me for what I did?"

To that, Stenog nodded. "You had no knowledge, of course. But our law has no clause about 'persons from another culture.' There is no other culture, no diversity whatever. Ignorant or not, you have to stand trial for sentence. There's a historic concept: Ignorance of the law is no excuse. And isn't that what you're claiming?"

The patent injustice of it staggered Parsons. Yet he could not tell from Stenog's tone just how serious the man was; the faintly detached, ironical quality could not be interpreted. Was Stenog mocking himself?"

Parsons said stiffly, "Can't you use your reason?"

Chewing his lip, Stenog said, "You have to abide by the laws of the community in which you live. Whether you came voluntarily or not. But"—He now appeared to be genuinely concerned; the irony had gone— "possibly some suspension can be worked out. The motions could be gone through."

Going from the room, he left Parsons alone for a time. When he returned he carried a polished oak box with a lock on it. Seating himself, he produced a key from his robe and unlocked the box. Out of it he lifted a massive white wig. With solemnity, he placed the wig on his head; at once, with his dark hair concealed, and the heavy rolls of the wig outlining his face, he lost the appearance of youth. A gravity and importance entered his appearance.

Stenog said, "As Director of the Fountain, I have the authority to pass judgment on you." From beneath his peruke, he scrutinized Parsons. "What we mainly have to consider is the formal procedure of exile."

"Exile!" Parsons echoed.

"We don't maintain our prison colonies here. I forget what system your culture employed. Work camps? C.C.C. in Soviet Asia?"

After a pause, Parsons managed to say. "By my time

the C.C.C. camps were gone. So were the slave labor camps in Russia."

"We make no attempt to rehabilitate the criminal," Stenog said. "That would be an invasion of his rights. And, from a practical standpoint, it doesn't work. We don't want substandard persons in our society."

"The *shupos*," Parsons said, with dread. "They're involved in these colonies?"

Stenog said, "The *shupos* are too valuable to be sent off Earth. A good deal of them are our youth, you understand. Especially the active element. The *shupo* organization maintains youth hostels and schools set apart from society, operated in the Spartan manner. The children are trained both in body and in mind. They're hardened. The activity that you saw, the raid on the illegal political group, is incidental, a sort of field expedition. They're quite zealous, the boys from the hostels. On the streets they have the right, as individuals, to challenge any person they feel is not acting properly."

"What are the prison colonies like?"

"They're city sized. You'll be free to work, and you'll have a separate dwelling of the apartment type where you can pursue various hobbies or creative crafts. The climate, of course, isn't favorable. Your life-span will be cut down enormously. Much depends on your own stamina."

"And there's no way I can appeal your decision?" Parsons demanded. "No trial system? The government brings the charges and then acts as the judge? Merely by putting on a medieval periwig—"

"We have the girl's signed complaint," Stenog said.

At that, Parsons stared at him. He could not believe it.

"Oh, yes," Stenog said. "Come along." Rising, he opened a side door, beckoning Parsons to follow him. formidable and solemn in his wig, he said, "Possibly this will tell you more about us than anything you have seen so far."

They passed by door after door; Parsons, in a daze, followed the bewigged younger man, barely able to keep up with his springy step. At last Stenog halted at a door, unlocked it, and stepped aside for Parsons to enter.

On the first of several small stages lay a body, partly covered by a white sheet. Icara. Parsons walked toward her. Her eyes were shut and she did not move. Her skin had a faded, washed-out quality.

"She filed the complaint," Stenog said, "just before she died." He switched on a light; gazing down. Parsons saw that beyond any doubt the girl was dead, possibly had been for several hours.

"But she was recovering," he said. "She was getting well."

Reaching down, Stenog lifted the sheet back. Along the side of the girl's neck, Parsons saw a careful, precise slash. The great carotid arteries had been cut, and expertly.

"In her complaint, she charged you with deliberately obstructing the natural process of seelmotus," Stenog said. "As soon as she had filled out this form she called her residential euthanor and underwent the Final Rite."

"Then she did it herself," Parsons said.

"It was her pleasure. By her own will she undid the harm you had attempted." Stenog shut off the light.

FIVE

IN HIS OWN personal car, Stenog took him to his house for dinner.

As they drove through the afternoon traffic, Parsons tried to see as much of the city as possible. Once, when the car halted for a three-level bus, he rolled down the window and leaned out. Stenog made no move to inhibit his actions.

"There's where I work," Stenog said once. He slowed the car and pointed. A flat building, larger than any others that Parsons had seen, lay to their right. "That's where we were—in my office at the Fountain. That means nothing to you, but you were at the most highly guarded spot we possess. We've been all this time getting through the check-stations." They had been in the car now for almost half an hour. "Every day I have to go through this," Stenog said. "And I'm the Director of the Fountain. But they check me, too."

A final uniformed guard halted the car, took the flat black card that Stenog showed him, and then the car started up onto a through ramp. The city fell below them.

"The Soul Cube is at the Fountain," Stenog said, by way of explanation. "But that makes no sense to you either, does it?"

"No," Parsons said. His mind was still on the girl, and on her death.

"Concentric rings," Stenog continued. "Zones of importance. Now, of course, we're out in the tribal areas again." The brightly colored dots that Parsons had first seen now passed by them at high velocity; Stenog did not appear to be a fast driver. In the daylight, Parsons noticed that each passing car had one of the tribal totem animals painted on its door, and, on the hoods, metal and plastic ornaments that might have been totem—the cars moved by too fast for him to be certain.

"You'll stay with me," Stenog said, "until time for your emigration to Mars. That should be in a day or so; it takes a little time to arrange transportation, what with all the red tape and government forms."

The house, small, part of a group of many houses built along the same lines, reminded Parsons of his own house. On the front steps he halted for a moment.

"Go ahead in," Stenog said. "The car parks itself." His hand on Parsons' shoulder, he steered him up the steps and onto the porch. The front door, open, let out the sound of music. "You lived before the age of radio, didn't you?" Stenog said as they entered.

"No," Parsons said. "We had it."

"I see," Stenog said. He seemed tired, now, at the end of the day. "Dinner should be ready," he murmured; sitting down on a long low couch he removed his sandals.

As Parsons moved about the living room he realized that Stenog was gazing at him oddly.

"Your shoes," Stenog said. "Didn't you people take off your shoes when you entered a house?"

After Parsons had removed his shoes Stenog clapped his hands. A moment later a woman appeared from the back of the house, wearing a flowing, brightly colored robe, her feet bare. She paid no attention to Parsons. From a low cabinet set against the wall she brought forth a tray on which stood a ceramic pot and a tiny glazed cup; Parsons smelled tea as the woman set the tray down on a table near the couch on which Stenog sat. Without a word, Stenog poured himself tea and began to drink.

None for me, Parsons thought. Because he was a criminal? Or were all guests treated this way? The differing customs. Stenog had not introduced the woman to him. Was she his wife? His maid?

Gingerly, Parsons seated himself on the far end of the couch. Neither Stenog nor the woman gave any sign that he had done rightly or wrongly; the woman kept her black eyes fixed on Stenog while he drank. She, too, like all the others Parsons had seen in this world, had the long shiny hair, the dark coloring; but in her he thought he saw one difference. This woman seemed less dainty, more heavily built.

"This is my *puella*," Stenog said, having finished his cup of tea. "Let's see." He relaxed, yawned, obviously glad to be out of his office and in his own home. "Well, there's probably no way I can express it to you. We have a legal relationship, recorded by the government. It's voluntary. I can break it; she can't." He added, "Her name is Amy."

The woman held out her hand to Parsons; he took it, and found himself shaking hands. This hadn't changed, this custom. The sense of continuity raised his morale slightly, and he found himself, too relaxing.

"Tea for Dr. Parsons," Stenog said.

While the two men sipped tea. Amy fixed dinner somewhere out of sight, behind a fragile-looking screen that Parsons recognized as distinctly Oriental. And here, as in his office, Stenog had a harpsichord; on this one stood a stack of sheet music, some of it very old looking.

After dinner, Stenog rose and said, "Let's take a run down to the Fountain." He nodded to Parsons. "I want you to understand out point of view."

Together, in Stenog's car, they drove through the night darkness. The air, fresh and cold, blew around Parsons; the younger man kept the windows down, clearly from habit. He seemed withdrawn into himself, and Parsons did not try to talk to him.

As they were being processed through the check-stations once more, Stenog abruptly burst out, "Do you consider this society morbid?"

"There are strains of it," Parsons said. "Visible to an outsider. The emphasis on death—"

"On life, you mean."

"When I first got here, the first person who saw me tried to run me down and kill me. Thinking I wanted to be killed." *And Icara*, he thought.

"That person probably saw you roaming around alone at night, on foot, on the public highway."

"Yes," Parsons said.

"That's one of the favorite ways for certain types of dashing individuals with a flair for the spectacular. They go out of the highway, outside the city, and it's the custom that the cars that see them run over them. It's time-honored, established. Didn't persons in your society go out at night, onto bridges, and throw themselves off?"

Parsons said, "But they were a trivial few, a mentally disturbed minority."

"Yet the custom, even so, was established within society! It was *understood*. If you decided to kill yourself, that was the proper way." Now, working himself up emotionally, Stenog said, "Actually, you know nothing about this society—you just came here. Look at this."

They had come out in a huge chamber. Parsons halted, impressed by the maze of corridors that stretched off in all directions. Even at night, work continued; the corridors were active and alight.

One wall of the chamber looked onto the edge of a cube. Going in that direction, Parsons discovered with a shock that he was seeing only a slice of the cube; virtually all of it lay buried in the ground, and he could only infer dimly what its full size might be.

The cube was alive.

The ceaseless undercurrent drummed up from the floor itself; he felt it moving through his body. An illusion, created by the countless technicians hurrying back and forth? Self-regulated freight elevators brought up empty containers, loaded themselves with new material and descended again. Armed guards prowled back and forth, keeping an eye on things; he saw them watching even Stenog. But the sense of life was not an illusion; he felt the emanation from the cube, the churning. A controlled, measured metabolism, but with a peculiar overtone of restlessness. Not a tranquil life, but with the tidal ebb and flow of the sea. Disturbing to him, and also to the other people; he caught, on their faces, the same fatigue and tension that he had seen with Stenog.

And he felt coldness rising from the cube.

Odd, he thought. Alive and cold . . . not like our life, not warm. In fact, he could see the breaths of the individuals in the corridors, his own, Stenog's, the white fog blown out by each of them. The pneuma.

"What is in it?" he asked Stenog.

Stenog said, "We are."

At first, he did not understand; he assumed the man meant it metaphorically. Then, by degrees, he began to see.

"Zygotes," Stenog said. "Arrested and frozen in cold-pack by the hundred billion. Our total seed. Our horde. The *race* is in there. Those of us now walking around—" He made a motion of dismissal. "A minute fraction of what's contained in there, the future generations to come."

So, Parsons thought, their minds aren't fixed on the present; it's the future that's real to them. Those to come, in a sense, are more real than those who are walking around now.

"How is it regulated?" he asked Stenog.

"We keep a constant population. Roughly, two and three-quarter billion. Each death automatically starts a new zygote from cold-pack along its regular developmental path. For each death there is an instantaneous new life; the two are interwoven."

Parsons thought. So out of death comes life. In their view, death is the cause of life.

"Where do the zygotes come from?" he inquired.

"Contributed according to a specific and very complex pattern. Each year we have Lists. Contest examinations between the tribes. Tests that cover all phases of ability, physical fitness, mental faculties, and intuitive functioning at every level and of every description and orientation. From the most abstract to the object-correlatives, the manual skills."

With comprehension, Parsons said, "The contribution of gametes is proportional to the test ratings of each tribe."

Stenog nodded. "In the last Lists the Wolf Tribe gained sixty victories out of two hundred. Therefore it contributed thirty percent of the zygotes for the next period, more than the three next highest-scoring tribes. As many gametes as possible are taken from the actual high-scoring men and women. The zygotes are always formed here, of course. Unauthorized zygote formation is illegal . . . but I don't want to offend your sensibilities. Extremely talented persons have made substantial contributions, even where their particular tribes have scored low. Once a gifted individual is located, all efforts are made to obtain his or her total supply of gametes. The Mother Superior of the Wolf Tribe, for example. None of Loris' gametes are lost. Each is removed as it is formed and immediately impregnated at the Fountain. Inferior gametes, the seed of low-scores, are ignored and allowed to perish."

Now, with first real clarity, Parsons grasped the underlying scheme of this world. "Then your stock is always improving."

"Of course," Stenog said, surprised.

"And the girl, Icara. She wanted to die because she was maimed, disfigured. She knew she would have had to compete in the Lists that way."

"She would have been a negative factor. She was what we call substandard. Her tribe would have been pulled down by her entry. But as soon as she was dead, a superior zygote, from a later stock than her own, was released. And at the same time a nine month embryo was brought out and severed from the Soul Cube. A Beaver died. Therefore this new baby will wear the emblem of the Beaver Tribe. It will take Icara's place."

Parsons nodded slowly. "Immortality." Then death,

he realized, has a positive meaning. Not the end of life. And not merely because these people *wish* to believe, but because *it is a fact*. Their world is constructed that way.

This is no idle mysticism! he realized. *This is their science.*

On the drive back to Stenog's house, Parsons contemplated the bright-eyed men and women along the route. Strong noses and chins. Clear skins. A handsome race of imposing men and full-breasted young women, all in the prime of youth. Laughing, hurrying through their fine city.

He caught a glimpse, once, of a man and woman passing along a spidery ramp, a strand of shimmering metal connecting two spires. Neither of them was over twenty. Holding hands as they rushed along, talking and smiling at each other. The girl's small, sharply-etched face, slender arms, tiny feet in sandals. A rich face, full of life and happiness. And health.

Yet, this was a society built on death. Death was an everyday part of their lives. Individuals died and no one was perturbed, not even the victims. They died happily, gladly. But it was wrong. It was against nature. A man was supposed to defend his life instinctively. Place it before everything else. This society denied a basic drive common to all life forms.

Struggling to express himself, he said, "You invite death. When someone dies, you're glad."

"Death," Stenog said, "is part of the cycle of existence, as much so as birth. You saw the Soul Cube. A man's death is as significant as his life." He spoke disjointedly, as traffic ahead of him caused him to turn his attention back to driving.

And yet, Parsons thought, this man does everything he can to avoid piling up his car. He's a careful driver. A contradiction.

In my own society—

Nobody thought about death. The system in which he had been born, in which he had grown up, had no explanation for death. A man simply lived out his life and tried to pretend that he wouldn't die.

Which was more realistic? This integration of death into the society, or the neurotic refusal of his own society to consider death *at all*? Like children, he decided. Unable and unwilling to imagine their own deaths . . . that's how my world operated. Until mass death caught up with us all, as apparently it did.

"Your forefathers," Stenog said, "the early Christians, I mean, hurled themselves under chariot wheels. They sought death, and yet out of their beliefs came your society."

Parsons said slowly. "We may ignore death, we may immaturely *deny* the existence of death, but at least we don't court death."

"You did indirectly," Stenog said. "By denying such a powerful reality, you undermined the rational basis of your world. You had no way to cope with war and famine and overpopulation because you couldn't bring yourselves to discuss them. So war *happened* to you; it was like a natural calamity, not man-made at all. It became a force. We control our society. We contemplace all aspects of our existence, not merely the good and pleasant."

For the rest of the trip they drove in silence.

After they had gotten out of the car, and had started up the front steps of the house, Stenog paused at a shrub that grew by the porch. In the porchlight he directed Parsons' attention to the various blooms.

"What do you notice growing?" he said, lifting a heavy stalk.

"A bud."

Stenog lifted another stalk. "And here is a blooming flower. And over here, a dying flower. Past its bloom." He took a knife from his belt and with one swift, clean swipe he severed the dying flower from the shrub and dropped it over the railing. "You saw three things: the bud, which is the life to come. The blossom, which is the life going on now. And the dead flower, which I cut off so that new buds could form."

Parsons was deep in thought. "But somewhere in this world, there's someone who doesn't think like you do. That must be why I was brought here. Sooner or later—"

"They'll show up?" Stenog finished, his face animated.

All at once Parsons understood why no attempt had been made to keep him under careful guard. Why Stenog drove him so openly and readily about the city, brought him to his house, to the Fountain itself.

They *wanted* the contact made.

Inside the house, in the living room, Amy sat at the harpsichord. At first the music did not seem familiar to Parsons, but after a time he became aware that she was playing Jelly Roll Morton tunes, but in some strange, inaccurate rhythm.

"I got to looking for something from your period," she said, pausing. "You didn't happen ever to see Morton, did you? We consider him on a par with Dowland and Schubert and Brahms."

Parsons said, "He lived before my time."

"Am I doing it wrong?" she said, noticing his expression. "I've always been fond of music of that period. In fact, I did a paper on it, in school."

"Too bad I can't play," he said. "We had TV, in our period. Learning to play a musical instrument had just about vanished as either a social or a cultural experience." In fact, he had never played a musical instrument of any kind; he recognized the harpsichord only from having seen one in a museum. This culture had revived elements from centuries previous to his own, had made them a part of their world; for him, music had been important, but it had come from recordings, or, at best, concerts. The idea of playing music in the home was as incredible as owning one's own telescope.

"I'm surprised you don't play," Stenog said. He had produced a bottle and glasses. "What about this? Fermented drink, made from grains."

"I think I recall that," Parsons said with amusement.

Still very seriously, Stenog said, "As I understand it,

liquor was introduced to take the place of drugs popular during your period. It has fewer toxic side-effects than the drugs you're probably familiar with." He opened the bottle and began to pour. From the color and smell, Parsons guessed that the stuff was a sour-mash bourbon.

He and Stenog sat drinking, while Amy played her eerie version of Dixieland jazz at the harpsichord. The house had a deeply peaceful air, and he felt himself becoming a little more calm. Was this, after all, so vile a society?

How, he thought can a society be judged by an individual created by another society? There's no disinterested standard. I'm merely comparing this world to mine. Not to a third.

The bourbon seemed to his taste unaged; he drank only a little. Across from him, Stenog filled his own glass a second time, and now Amy came over. He watched her go to the cupboard for a glass; Stenog had not gotten one out for her. The status of women . . . and yet, in his contact with Wade and Icara, he had not been conscious of this disparity.

"That illegal political group," he said. "What did they advocate?"

Stenog stirred. "Voting rights for women."

Although she had her drink, Amy did not join them. She retired to a corner and seated herself, small and quiet and thoughtful.

But she did mention going to school, Parsons remembered. So women aren't excluded from educational opportunities. Perhaps education itself, especially non-scientific education, such as a degree in history, has no status here. Something appropriate for women: a mere hobby.

Studying his glass, Stenog said, "Do you like my *puella*?"

Embarrassed, Parsons said, "I—" He could not keep himself from glancing in her direction. She showed no emotion.

"You're staying here tonight," Stenog said. "You can sleep with Amy if you want."

To that, Parsons could say nothing. Guardedly, he looked from Stenog to Amy, trying to make out what actually was meant. Here, the language barrier had betrayed him—and the difference in customs.

"That's not done in my time segment," he said finally.

"Well, you're here now," Stenog said with a touch of ire.

Certainly, that was true. Parsons considered, and then said, "I should think this practice would upset your careful control of zygote formation."

At once, both Stenog and Amy started. "Oh," Amy said. "Of course." To Stenog she said, "Remember, he didn't go through the Initiation." With visible uneasiness she added, "It's a good thing he spoke up. This could be a very dangerous situation. I'm surprised none of you thought about it."

Drawing himself up, Stenog said with pride, "Parsons, prepare to have your sensibilities offended."

"That isn't important," Amy said to him. "I'm thinking of situations he might get into."

Paying no attention to her, Stenog focused his attention on Parsons. "All males are sterilized at the inception of puberty," he said, an expression of deep satisfaction on his face. "Myself, included."

"So you can see," Amy said, "why this custom causes no particular trouble. But in your case—"

"No, no," Stenog said. "You can't sleep with her, Parsons. In fact, you can't sleep with any of the women." Now he, too, had become disturbed. "You should be gotten to Mars, I think. As soon as it's feasible. A thing like this . . . it could cause great problems."

Approaching Parsons, Amy said, "More to drink?" She started to refill his glass. He did not protest.

SIX

It became feasible at four that morning. Suddenly Jim Parsons found himself on his feet, out of bed; his clothes were handed to him, and before he had even gotten half-dressed the several men, wearing government uniforms of some kind, had him in motion, out of the house to a parked car. No one spoke to him. The men worked fast, and with skill. A moment later the car carried him at high speed along the empty highway, away from the city.

At no time did he see any sign of Stenog. Or of Amy.

The field, when they reached it, surprised him by its size: no larger than the back yard of an ordinary upper-middle-class home, and not even fully level. On it a ship, like an egg, painted originally a dark blue but not pitted and corroded, was in the process of being prepared. Several field lights had been trained on it, and in the glare technicians were going over it, making what he guessed to be final examinations.

Almost at once he found himself being propelled up a ramp and through the porthole entrance of the ship. There, in a single compartment, he was seated in a reinforced chair, slamped so that he could not stir—and at that point the men let go of him.

The compartment contained, besides himself, a single entity. He had never seen such an object before; he stared at it, feeling a pervasive dread.

The machine stood almost as high as a man, built

partly of opaque metals and plastic, and partly—near the top—of a transparent membrane through which he could see activity taking place. In a fluid, something soft, on the order of gray organic material, floated. Out of the top of the machine several delicate projections sprouted, reminding him of the below-surface portions of mushrooms. Fine interlacing of fibres almost too tenuous to be visible.

Pausing at the entrance porthole, one of the government men turned and said, "It's not alive. That business floating around up top, that's a section cut out of a rat brain. It's growing in the medium, but it's not conscious; it's just to simplify building them.

"Easier to cut a section from a rat brain than build a control," another man said, and then both of them disappeared; the lock slipped into place and the hull of the ship became sealed.

Immediately the machine in front of Parsons whirred, clicked, and said in a calm, distinctly human voice, "The trip to the Martian settlements takes approximately seventy-five minutes. You will be supplied with adequate ventilation and heat, but there is no provision for food except in emergency."

The machine clicked off. It had spoken its piece.

Now the ship shuddered. Parsons shut his eyes as the ship began to lift, very slowly at first, and then, abruptly, at enormous speed. The far section of wall had a wide slot for viewing purposes; he saw the surface of Earth rush away, the stars swirl as the ship changed course. Nice of them to let me see, he thought in a dazed, remote way.

Now the machine spoke again. "This ship is so constructed that tampering with any portion of it will produce a detonation that will destroy both the ship and occupant. The trajectory of flight is prearranged, and any tampering with the automatic self-contained beam will cause the same detonating mechanism to become active." After a moment the machine repeated its message.

The swirl of stars that he faced gradually settled

down. One spot of light began to grow, and he identified it as Mars.

"By your left hand you will find an emergency button," the machine said suddenly. "If you find yourself deprived of either adequate ventilation or warmth, press that button."

For other kinds of situations, Parsons thought, there probably are no provisions. This ship carries me to Mars, blows up if anyone tries to interfere, gives me air and heat, and that's its job.

The interior, as well as the exterior, had a worn, used quality. It's made this trip many times, he decided. It's carried quite a few people between Earth and the Martian settlements. Back and forth. A shuttle-service, leaving at odd hours.

Mars continued to grow. He guessed at the time. Half an hour possibly had gone by. It makes good speed, he thought. Perfected.

And then Mars, on the screen, disappeared.

The stars leaped; he felt a vacuum within him, as if he were falling. The stars settled into place and the feeling departed almost as quickly as it had come.

But, on the screen, he saw no destination. Only black emptiness and the far-off stars. The ship continued to move, but now he had no constant by which to measure.

Across from him, the machine clicked and said in its recorded human voice. "We have passed approximately half-way on the trip."

Something has gone wrong, Parsons realized. *This ship is no longer heading toward Mars*. And it did not seem to bother the robot self-regulating mechanism.

He thought in panic, *Mars is gone*!

Slightly over half an hour later the machine announced, "We are about to land. Be prepared for a series of concussions as the ship adjusts itself."

Beyond the ship—only void.

This is what they had in mind, Parsons thought. Stenog and the government men. No intention of taking me to any "prison colonies." This is a shuttle that drops me off to die, out in space.

"We have landed," the machine said. And then it corrected itself. "We are about to land." Several humming sounds issued from it and, although the voice had the same measured confidence, Parsons had the intuition that the machine, too, had been thrown off. Perhaps this situation hadn't been intentional—at least, not intended by the designers of the ship.

It's confused, he realized. It doesn't know what to do.

"This isn't Mars," Parsons said aloud. But, even as he spoke, he realized that it couldn't hear him; it was only a self-regulating device, not alive. "We're in the void," he said.

The machine said, "From here on you will be remanded to the local authorities. The trip is over." It feel silent then; he saw its swirling interior die off into immobility. It had done its job—or at least it imagined that it had done its job.

The entrance lock of the ship swung back, and Parsons gazed out into nothingness. Around him, the atmosphere of the ship began to shriek away, rushing out through the open lock. At once, a helmetlike unit sprang from the chair to which he was strapped; the unit dropped into his lap. And, at the same time, the machine returned to life.

"Emergency," the machine said. "Immediately don the protective equipment which has been put within your reach. Do not delay!"

Parsons did so. The straps that held him barely permitted him to get the unit into place. As the last air rushed from the ship, he had the unit over him. Already it had begun pumping; he tasted the stale, cool air.

The walls of the ship glowed red. Undoubtedly, an emergency mechanism was trying to make up for the dissipating heat.

For what he judged to be fifteen minutes the lock of

the ship remained open. Then, all at once, the lock slid shut.

Across from him the machine clicked, and inside it the sentient tissue eddied about in its medium. But the machine had nothing to say. No passengers go back, he decided. The ship shuddered, and, through the viewing slot, he saw a flash of light. Some kind of jets had gone into action.

With horror he realized that he was on his way across space once more. From one empty point to another. How many times? Would it go on and on, this meaningless shuttle-service?

Through the viewing slot the stars altered positions as the ship adjusted itself onto its return course. Hope entered him. Maybe, at the other end, he would find Earth. Through some mechanical failure the ship had taken him, not to Mars, but to a random, alternate point; but now the mistake would be rectified. Now he would find himself back where he had started.

Seventy-five minutes later—at least, he presumed it to be—the ship shuddered and once again unfastened its entrance lock. Once more he gazed out into the void. Oh, God, he thought. And not even the physical sense of motion; only the intellectual realization that I have traveled between far-distant points. Millions and millions of miles.

After a time the lock slid shut. Again, he thought. The nightmare. The terrible dream of motion. If he shut his eyes, did not look at the viewing slot, and if he could keep his mind from working . . .

That would be insanity, he decided.

How easy it would be. To sink into an insane withdrawal, sitting here in this chair. Ignore what I know to be true.

But in a few more hours he would be hungry. Already his mouth had become dry; he would die of thirst long before he died of hunger.

The machine said in the calm voice so familiar to him now, "The trip to the Martian settlements takes approximately seventy-five minutes. You will be supplied with adequate ventilation and heat, but there is no provision for food except in emergency."

Isn't this an emergency? Parsons thought. Will it recognize it as such? When I begin to die of thirst, perhaps?

Will it squirt me with water from taps somewhere in the walls of the ship? Across from him the bit of gray rat tissue floated in its medium. You're not alive, Parsons said to himself. You're not suffering; you're not even aware of this.

He thought about Stenog. Did you plan this? I can't believe it. This is some hideous freak accident. Nobody planned this.

Someone took away Mars and the Earth, he thought. And forgot about me. Take me too, he thought. Don't forget me; I want to go along.

The machine clicked and said, "This ship is so constructed that tampering with any portion of it will produce a detonation."

He felt a surge of bizarre hope. Better if the ship blew up, than this. Perhaps he could get loose . . . anything would be better.

In the viewing slot, the distant stars. Nothing to notice him.

While he stared at the viewing slot, a star detached itself. It was not a star. It was an object.

The object grew.

Coming closer, Parsons thought. For what seemed to him an unbearable time the object remained virtually the same size, not getting either larger or smaller. He could not tell what it was. A meteor? Bit of space debris? A ship? Keeping its distance . . .

The machine said, "We are about to land. Be prepared for a series of concussions as the ship adjusts itself."

This time, Parsons thought, something is out there. Not Mars. Not a planet. But—something.

"We are going to land," the machine said, and, as before, began a rapid series of uncertain noises. "We have landed," it said at last.

The lock slid open. Again the void. Where is it?

Parsons asked silently. Has it gone? He could do nothing but sit, strapped to his chair. Please, he prayed. Don't go away.

In the entrance lock an opaque surface dropped into place, blocking the sight of stars.

"Help," Parsons shouted. His voice rebounded deafeningly in his helmet.

A man appeared, wearing a helmet that made him look like a giant frog. Without hesitation he sprinted toward Parsons. A second man followed him. Expertly, obviously knowing exactly what to do, they began cutting through the straps that held him to the chair. Sparks from the seared metal showered throughout the ship—and then they had him loose.

"Hurry," one of the men said, touching his helmet against Parsons' to make a medium for his voice. "It's open only a few more minutes."

Parsons, struggling painfully up, said, "What went wrong?"

"Nothing," the man said, helping him. The other, holding what Parsons recognized as a weapon, prowled about the ship watchfully. "We couldn't show up on Earth," the first man said, as he and Parsons moved toward the lock. "They were waiting—the *shupos* are good at it. We moved this ship back into time."

On the man's face, Parsons saw the grin of triumph. He and the man started from the ship, through the open lock. Not more than a hundred feet away a larger ship, like a pencil, hung waiting, its lock open, lights gleaming out. A cord connected the two ships.

Beside Parsons, his companion turned back for the other man. "Be careful," the man said to Parsons. "You're not experienced in crossing. Remember, no gravity. You could sail off." He clung to the cable, beckoning to his colleague.

His colleague took a step toward the lock. From the wall of the ship the muzzle of a gun appeared; the muzzle flashed orange, and the man pitched forward on his face. Beside Parsons, his companion gasped. His eyes met Parsons'. For an instant Parsons saw the man's face, distended with fear and comprehension;

then the man had lifted a weapon and fired directly at the blank wall of the ship, at the spot where the gun muzzle had appeared.

A blinding pop made Parsons fall back. The helmet of the man beside him burst; bits of helmet cascaded against his own. And, at the same time, the far wall of the ship splintered; a crack formed and material rained in all directions.

Exposed, but obviously already dying, a *shupo* confronted Parsons. The dwarf figure gyrated slowly, in an almost ritualistic convulsion. The eyes bulged, and then the *shupo* collapsed. Its damaged body floated and eddied about the ship, mixing with the clouds of particles. Finally it came to rest against the ceiling, head down, arms dangling grotesquely. Blood from the wound in its chest gathered in an elongated ball of glistening, bright crimson that froze, expanded, and, as it drifted against the *shupo's* leg, broke apart.

In Parsons' numbed brain the words that he had so recently heard returned. "*The* Shupos *are good at it.*" Yes, he thought. Very good. The *shupo* had been aboard all the time. It made no sound. Had not moved. Had gone on waiting. Would it have died there, in the wall, if no one had appeared?

Both men lay dead. The *shupo* had killed them both.

Beyond the prison ship the pencil-shaped ship still drifted at the end of its cable. Lights still gleamed out. But now it's empty, Parsons realized. They came for me, but too soon; they couldn't avoid the trap.

I wonder who they were.

Will I ever know?

Kneeling down, he started to examine the dead man nearest him. And then he remembered the lock. Any moment it would close—he would be sealed in here, and the ship would start back once more. Abandoning the two dead men he jumped through the lock, grasping the cable. His leap carried him farther than he had anticipated; for a moment he spun, sweeping away from the two ships, seeing them dwindle away from him. The bitter cold of space licked at him; he felt it seeping into his body. Struggling, he reached out, stretching his arms, fingers . . .

By degrees his body drifted toward the pencil-shaped ship. Suddenly it swept up at him; he smashed against it stunningly, and clung, spread out against its hull. Then, when his mind cleared, he began moving inch-by-inch toward the open entrance.

His fingers touched the cable. He dragged himself down and inside the ship. Warmth from the ship spread around him, and the chill began to depart.

Across the cable-length, at the far end, the entrance lock of the prison ship clicked shut.

Kneeling, Parsons found the origin of the cable. How firmly was it attached? Already, the prison ship's rockets had begun to fire; it was ready to start back. The cable became taut; the prison ship was pulling against it.

In panic, Parsons thought. *Do I want to go back? Or should I cut the cable?*

But the decision had been made. As the rockets fired, the cable snapped. The police ship, at terrific speed, shot away, became small, and then vanished.

Gone. Back to Earth. Carrying three corpses.

And where was he?

Closing the door by hand—it took considerable effort, but at last he had it in place—Parsons turned to examine the ship into which he had come. The ship that had been intended as his means of rescue, and which, for all practical purposes, had failed.

SEVEN

ON ALL SIDES of him, meters and controls. The central panel glowed with data.

Parsons seated himself on one of two stools facing the panel. In an ash tray he saw a smoldering cigarette butt. Only a few minutes ago the two men had hurried out of here, across to the prison ship; now they were dead, and now he was here in their place.

He thought, *Am I much better off?*

The control panel hummed. Dials changed slightly. The man had said, *"We moved the ship back in time."* How far in time?

But also, it must travel in space. It goes in both dimensions.

Examining the controls, he wondered. Which operates which? He could make out a division on the board, two hemispheres.

Somebody *was* trying to reach me, he realized. They brought me forward through time, hundreds of years. From my society to theirs. For some purpose. Will I ever know the purpose?

At least I saw them face to face. If only for a moment.

Good God, he thought. I'm lost in space and I'm lost in time. In both dimensions.

Above the hum of the panel he detected an intermittent crackle of static. Now he located the cloth grill of a speaker. A communication system? But connected to what?

Reaching out, he experimentally turned a knob. Nothing appreciable changed. He pressed a button near the edge of the board.

All the dials changed.

Around him the ship trembled. The muffled concussion of jets shook him. We're moving, he thought. Hands swept out clock-faces, counters vanished; no numbers at all showed. A red light winked on, and at once the dials slowed.

Some safety mechanism had come on.

The viewscreen over the controls showed stars. But now one bright dot had become larger. He saw in its color a clear tint of red. A planet. Mars?

Taking a deep, unsteady breath, he once again began experimenting with the controls.

Below him a parched red plain stretched out.

He did not recognize it.

Far to the right—mountains. Cautiously, he tried adjustments. The ship dropped sharply; he managed to steady it until it hung above the sun-cracked land. Corrosion . . . he saw limitless furrows gouged into the baked clay. Nothing moved. No life.

After many failures he managed to land the ship. With care he unbolted the door.

An acrid wind billowed into the ship and around him. He sniffed the smell of age and erosion. But the air, thin and weak, brought a faint trickle of warmth. Now Parsons stepped out onto the crumbling sand; his feet sank and he stumbled.

For the first time in his life he was standing on another planet.

Scanning the sky he made out dim clouds on the horizon. Did he see a bird among them? Black speck that disappeared.

The silence frightened him.

He began to walk. Beneath his feet, stones broke

apart and puffed into particles. No water! Bending, he picked up a handful of sand. Rough against his skin.

To his right, a heap of slag and boulders.

There, in the cold shadows, gray lichens that seemed no more than stains on the rock. He climbed the largest of the boulders. Far off he saw what might have been an artificial construction. The remains of some massive trench cut deep into the desert. So he went that way.

He thought, I'd better not lose sight of the ship.

While he walked he saw his second sign of life. On his wrist, a fly. It danced off and disappeared. Most noxious of all pests, and yet preferable to the dead wastes. This meager life form, awesome and tragic in this context.

Yet surely if a fly could survive, there had to be organic matter.

Possibly on some other part of the planet, a settlement of some kind. The prison colonies—unless he had arrived long before or long after. Once he had mastered the controls of the ship . . .

In the distance, something sparkled.

He started in that direction. At last he came close enough to make out the sight of an upright slab. A marker? Breathless, he went up a slope, sliding in the loose sand.

In the weak, ruddy sunlight he saw before him a granite block set in the sand. Green patina covered it, almost obscuring that which had flashed: a metal plate bolted to the center.

On the plate—writing. Engraved deep into the metal at one time, but now scoured almost smooth. Squatting down, he tried to read. Most of it was obliterated or illegible, but at the top, in larger letters, a word that could still be read:

PARSONS

His own name. Coincidence? He stared at it, unbelieving. Then, pulling off his shirt, be began rubbing away the accumulation of sand and grime. Before his name, another word:

JIM

So there could be no doubt. This plaque, set here in this wasteland, had him as its topic. Into his mind came the mad, eerie notion that perhaps he had become some gigantic figure in history, known to all the planets. A legendary figure, commemorated in this monument, like some god.

But now, feverishly rubbing with his shirt, he managed to read the smaller engraving beneath. The plaque did not concern him; it was addressed to him. Foolishly, he sat in the sand, brushing at the letters.

The plaque told him how to operate the ship. A manual of instruction.

Each sentence was repeated, apparently to combat the ravages of time. He thought, they must have known that this block would stand here for centuries, perhaps thousands of years. Until I came along.

The shadows, on the far range of mountains, had become longer. Overhead, the sun had begun to decline. The day was ending. Now the air had lost all warmth. He shivered.

Gazing up at the sky he saw a shape half-lost in the haze. A gray disc sailed beyond the clouds. For a long time he watched it, his heart beating heavily. A moon, crossing the face of this world. Much closer than the Moon he knew; but perhaps its greater size was due to Mars being so much smaller. Shading his eyes against the long rays of the sun, he studied the face of this moon. The worn surface . . .

The moon was Luna.

That had not changed; the pattern on its visible side remained the same. This was not Mars. It was Earth.

Here he stood on his own planet, on the dying, ancient Earth. The waterless last age. It had, like Mars before it, ended in drought and weariness. With only black sand-flies and lichens. And rock. Probably it had been like this a long time, long enough to eradicate most of the remains of the human civilization that once existed. Only this plaque, erected by time travelers like himself; persons in search of him, tracking him down to re-establish the contact that had been lost. They had possibly put up many of these markers here and there.

His name, the final written words. To survive man, when everything else had gone.

At sunset he returned to the ship. Before entering it he paused, taking a last look behind him.

Better this, the night falling obscuring the plain. He could imagine animals stirring, night insects appearing.

Finally he shut the lock. He snapped on lights; the cabin of the ship filled with pale white, and the control panel glowed red. Overhead the loudspeaker crackled faintly to itself. The semblance, at least, of something alive.

And on the threshold, a creature that had crawled into the ship during his absence. A hard-to-kill form of life. An earwig.

He thought. That may survive everything else. The last to die. He watched this particular earwig crawl under a storage cupboard.

A few will probably still survive, he reflected, when the plaque with my name on it has crumbled to dust.

Seated at the controls he selected the keys which the instructions had described. Then, in the combination given him, he punched out the tape and started the transport feeding.

Dials changed.

Now he had turned control over to them, the people who wanted him. He sat passive as the odd shudder again reached him, and, on the viewing screen, the nocturnal scene jumped. Daylight returned, and, after a time, hues of green and blue to replace the parched red.

Earth reborn, he thought somberly. The desert made fertile once more. Faster and faster the scenes blurred, altered. Thousands of years passing backward, no doubt millions. He could scarcely grasp it. In his attempts to operate the ship he had run out the string entirely; he had gone into the future as far as the ship was capable of carrying him.

Abruptly, the dials ceased their motion.

I'm back, Parsons thought. Reaching out his hand, he touched a switch on the panel. The machinery shut off. He rose and walked to the door of the ship. For a moment he hesitated. And then he unbolted the door and pushed it wide.

A man and woman faced him. Each held a gun pointed at him. He caught a glimpse of a lush green landscape, trees and a building, flowers. The man said, "Parsons?" Golden, hot sunlight streamed down.

"Yes," he said.

"Welcome," the woman said in a husky, throaty voice. But the guns did not lower. "Come out of the ship, Doctor," the woman said.

He did so.

"You found one of those markers?" the man said. "The instructions sent ahead for you?"

Parsons said, "Apparently it had been up a long time."

Going by him, the woman entered the ship. She inspected the meter readings on the panel. "A very long time," she said. To her companion, she said, "Helmar, he went all the way."

"You're lucky it was still usable," the man said.

"Are you going to keep the guns pointed at me?" Parsons said.

The woman came to the doorway behind him and said over his shoulder, "I don't see any *shupos*. I think it's all right." She had put her gun away already, and now the man did so too.

The man put his hand out; he and Parsons shook.

"Do women shake hands too?" the woman asked, extending her hand. "I hope this doesn't violate a custom of your period."

The man—Helmar—said, "How did the far future strike you?"

"I couldn't take it," Parsons said.

"It's quite depressing," Helmar said. "But remember; it'll be a long time coming, and gradual. And by that time there'll be other planets inhabited." Both he and the woman regarded him with expressions of deep emotion. And he, too, felt profoundly moved.

"Care for a drink, Doctor?" the woman asked.

"No," he said. "Thanks." He saw bees at work in nearby vines, and, further along, a row of cypress trees. The man and woman followed after him as he walked in the direction of the trees. Halfway there he halted, taking in deep lungsful of air. The pollen-laden air of midsummer . . . the odors of growing things.

"Time travel works erratically," the woman said. "At least for us. We've had bad luck striving for exactitude. I'm sorry."

"That's all right," Parsons said.

Now he surveyed the man and woman, aware of them more clearly.

The woman was beautiful even beyond what he had already seen in this world of youth and robust bodies. This woman was *different.* Copper-colored skin that shone in the midday sun. The familiar flat cheek bones and dark eyes, but a different kind of nose. Stronger. All her features had an emphatic quality new to his experience. And she was older. Perhaps in her middle thirties. A powerfully built creature, with cascades of black hair, a heavy torrent all the way down her shoulders to her waist.

On the front of her robe, lifted high by her breasts, was a herald, an intricate design woven into the rich fabric, that rose and fell with the motion of her breathing. A wolf's head.

"You're Loris," Parsons said.

"That's right," the woman answered.

He could see why she had become the Mother Superior of the society. Why her contribution to the Soul Cube was of supreme importance. He could see it in her eyes, in the firm lines of her body, her wide forehead.

Beside her, the man shared some of her characteristics. The same coppery skin, the starkly etched nose, the mass of black hair. But with subtle, crucial differences. A mere mortal, Parsons thought. Yet even so, impressive. Two fine and handsome individuals, returning his gaze with intelligence and sympathy, alert to his needs. A high emphatic order, he decided. Their dark eyes had a depth to which he felt his own psyche respond; the strength of their personalities forced his, too, to rise to a higher level of cognition.

To him Helmar said, "Let's go inside." He indicated the gray stone building nearby. "It's cooler, and we can sit down."

As they walked up the path, Loris said, "And more private."

A collie, wagging its great tail, approached them, its elongated muzzle raised. Helmar paused to thump the dog. As they turned the corner of the building, Parsons saw descending terraces, a well-tended garden that merged with trees and wilder shrubs.

"We're quite secluded here," Loris said. "This is our Lodge. It dates back three hundred years."

In the center of an open field, Parsons saw a second time travel ship and several men at work on it.

"You may be interested in this," Loris said. Leading the way, she brought Parsons over to the ship; there she took a smooth, shiny sphere from one of the technicians. The sphere, the size of a grapefruit, lifted of its own accord from her hands; she caught hold of it at once. "It's all set to go," she said. "We're in the process of taking these into the future." She pointed; the ship had been filled with these spheres.

Helmar said, "I presume by the time you came onto it, the thing was rather shabby looking."

Parsons took the sphere from Loris. "I don't recognize it," he said, examining it.

Helmar and Loris exchanged glances. "These are the markers," Loris said. "One of these contacted you in the far future."

"These transmit for hundreds of miles," Helmar said. "To your ship's radio." They both stared at him. "Didn't you get your instructions through the loudspeaker? Didn't you hear one of these telling you how to operate the ship to bring it back here?"

"No," Parsons said. "I found a granite monument with a metal plaque. The instructions were engraved in the metal."

Silence.

At last Loris said quietly, "We know nothing about that. We constructed no such device. And it gave you *instructions*?"

Helmar said, "For operating our time ship?"

"Yes," Parsons said. "And it was addressed to me. It had my name on it."

Helmar said, "We've sent out hundreds of these markers. You never encountered *one*?"

"No," Parsons said.

The man and woman had lost their air of confidence. And Parsons, too, wondered the same thing. What had become of these spheres? And, if these people hadn't erected the plaque, *then who had*?

EIGHT

PARSONS SAID, "Why did you bring me to your time?"

After a pause, Loris said, "We have a medical problem. We've tried to solve it, but we've failed. More accurately, we've had only a limited success. Our medical knowledge falls short, and in our world there's no better knowledge that we can draw on."

"How many of you are there?" Parsons said.

Loris smiled. "Just ourselves and a few others. A few who are sympathetic."

"Within your tribe?"

"Yes," she said.

"What will the government think happened to me? They know something happened to the prison rocket."

"The rocket disappeared," Helmar said. "Very common. That's why the prisoner is sent unescorted. Travel between planets is as erratic as time travel. Like the early days of travel between Europe and the New World . . . tiny ships setting out into the void."

Parsons said, "But they'll suspect that—"

"Suspecting is not the same as knowing," Loris said. "What information does it give them about us? Not even that we exist, let alone who we are or what we are trying to do. At best, they know no more than they did already."

"Then they do suspect you," Parsons said. "Already."

"The government suspects that someone has been

able to make use of the time-travel experiments which they abandoned. Our early efforts were unfortunate. We dumped telltale material where they could find it and study it. They've had clues for some time." Her fierce, compelling eyes blazed. "But they wouldn't dare accuse me. They can't come here; this is sacred land. Our land. Our Lodge." Under her robes her breasts rose and fell.

Parsons said, "Is this medical problem getting worse while we stand here?"

"No," Helmar said. "We've managed to bring it to a stasis." His calm came as a contrast to Loris' fervor. "Remember, Doctor, *we have gained control of time.* If we're careful, no one can defeat us. We have a unique advantage."

"No group in history," Loris breathed, "has ever had our weapon, our opportunity."

As the three of them entered the Wolf Lodge, ascending a flight of wide stairs, Parsons thought to himself, But one of the principal discoveries in science is the demonstration that a thing is possible. Once that's been done, then half the work is over. These people have proved to the government that a time-travel machine can be built. The government now knows that it made an error in dropping its experiments. It doesn't know *how* the experiments were successfully completed, or by whom. But it does know—or at least, has good reason to presume—that time travel is possible. And that alone is a uniquely important discovery.

Both Loris and Helmar strode ahead with such determination that Parsons got only a glimpse of the long, dark-paneled hall. A double door slid back, and he was led into a luxurious alcove. Helmar seated him in a leather-covered armchair, and then, with a flourish, placed an ash tray beside him—and a package of Lucky Strike cigarettes.

"From your century," Helmar said. "Correct?"

"Yes," Parsons said, with gratitude.

"What about a beer?" Helmar said. "We have several beers from your period, all ice cold."

"This is fine," Parsons said, lighting one of the cigarettes and inhaling with enjoyment.

Loris, seating herself opposite, said, "And we've brought magazines forward. And clothing. And a variety of objects, some of which we can't identify. Chance plays quite a role, as you might guess. The time dredge scoops up more than three tons; we often get mere debris, however, especially in the earlier stages." She also took one of the cigarettes.

"Have you been able to orient yourself to our world?" Helmar said, seating himself and crossing his legs.

Parsons said, "The government official I ran into—"

"Stenog," Loris said. Her face showed her aversion. "We know him. Technically, he's in charge of the Fountain, but we have reason to believe he's tied up with the *shupos*. Of course, he disavows that."

"They harness what would be delinquent children," Helmar said. "Putting their energies and talents at the disposal of the government. The desire to maim and kill and fight. They train the youth to have contempt for death, which, as you have learned, is a valuable point of view to have in our society." His eyes had a deep grimness in them.

"You must realize," Loris said, "that this society has been long established. This way of life has the sanction of years. This is not a momentary abnormality in history. Human beings are a cheap commodity in history; we've seen quite a panorama come and go, during our work with the dredge. It gives one a rather different point of view, to go back and forth into time. Both Helmar and I can see—at least intellectually—the tribes' concept of the inevitability of life. They do not encourage life in the same way as they encourage death. They limit birth, for instance, to achieve a static population."

Helmar said, "Had they not limited birth, there would be by now a valuable human population on Mars and Venus. But as you know, Mars is used only as a prison. Venus is used as a source of raw materials. Sapped, year after year. Plundered."

"As the New World was plundered by the Spanish and French and English," Loris said.

She pointed upward, and Parsons saw that along one wall of the room hung large framed portraits, ancient faces familiar to him. Portraits of Cortez, Pizarro, Drake, Cabrillo, and others that he could not manage to identify. But all wore the ruffles of the sixteenth century; all were noblemen and explorers of that period.

Those were the only pictures in the room.

"Why your interest in sixteenth century explorers?" he asked.

Loris said, "You'll learn about that in due time. The point which I mean to stress is this. Despite the morbid strain in this society, there is no reason to expect it to expire and decline from its own imbalances. Having looked ahead, we can see that there's a life expectancy for it of several centuries. We share your aversion to its dynamics, but—" She shrugged. "We're more stoic about it. As you will be, finally."

Rome, Parsons thought, didn't decline in a day.

"What about my own society?" he said.

"It depends on what you identify as the authentic values of your society. Some, of course, still survive and may always survive. The superiority of the white nations, Russia, Europe and North American democracies, lasted about a century after your time; then Asia and Africa emerged as the dominant areas, with the so-called 'colored' races acquiring their rightful heritage."

Helmar said, "In the wars of the twenty-third century, all races blended together, you understand. So, from that time on, it was not meaningful to speak of 'white' or 'colored' races."

"I see," Parsons said. "But the appearance of this Soul Cube, and these tribes—"

"That, of course," Loris said, "was not connected with the blending of the several races. The divisions into tribes is purely artificial, as you've probably concluded. It stems from a twenty-third century innovation, a great world-wide competition along the olympics line—but with the victors becoming eligible for national office. At that time, there were still nations, and the participants at first came as representations of their nations."

"The Communist youth festivals," Helmar said, "were one of the historic sources of the custom. And of course the medieval jousts."

Loris said, "But the principal origin of the Soul Cube, and the planned manipulation of zygotes, doesn't lie in any source that you would be aware of." Facing Parsons, her eyes intense, she said, "You must understand that for centuries the colored races of the world had been told they were inferior, that they couldn't control their own destinies. There is in all of us this lingering sense that we have to prove we're better, prove we're able to construct a society and a population far more advanced than any seen in the past."

Helmar said, "We've made our point, but we've achieved a calcified society that spends its time meditating about death; it has no plans, no direction. No desire for growth. Our nagging sense of inferiority has betrayed us; it's made us expend our energies in recovering our pride, in proving our ancient enemies false. Like the Egyptian society—death and life so interwoven that the world has become a cemetery, and the people nothing more than custodians living among the bones of the dead. They are virtually the pre-dead, in their own minds. So their great heritage has been frittered away. Think what they—we—might have become." He broke off, his face a study of conflicting emotions.

For a time none of them spoke, Then Parsons, eager to change the subject, said, "What's your medical problem?" He wanted, now, to see it at once. To find out what is was.

"Turn your chair," Loris said. She and Helmar turned until they faced the far wall of the room. Parsons did so, too.

Breathing quickly, her lips half-parted, her fists clenched at her sides, Loris stared at the wall.

"Watch," she said. She pressed a stud.

The wall dimmed. It flickered and was gone. Parsons found himself looking into another room. Familiar, he thought. A place he had been. Was it—the Fountain!

Not quite. Everything here was minute. This chamber was a replica of what he had seen at the Fountain. The same syndromes of equipment, power cables, freight elevators. And at the far end, the gleaming blank surface of a cube—a scaled down cube, perhaps ten feet high and three feet in depth.

"What is it?" Parsons demanded.

Loris hesitated.

"Go ahead," Helmar said.

Now she touched the stud again. The blank face of the cube faded. They were looking inside, into its depths. Into the swirling liquid that filled it.

A man stood upright, suspended in the medium of the cube. He lay motionless, arms at his sides, eyes shut. With a shock, Parsons realized that the man was dead. Dead—and somehow preserved within the cube. He was tall, powerfully built, with a great gleaming copper-colored torso. His nude body was maintained uncorrupted by this miniature Soul Cube, this small version of the great government cube at the Fountain.

Instead of a hundred billion zygotes and developed embryos, this small cube contained the preserved body of a single man, a fully developed male perhaps thirty years old.

"Your husband?" Parsons asked Loris, without thinking.

"No. We have no husbands." Loris gazed at the man with great emotion. She seemed in the grip of a swelling tide of feeling.

Parsons persisted. "You had an emotional relationship? He was your lover?"

Loris shuddered, then abruptly laughed. "No, not my lover." Her whole body swayed, trembled, as she rubbed her forehead and turned away a moment. "Although we have lovers, of course. Quite a few. Sexual activity continues, independent of reproduction." She seemed almost in a trance. Her words came slowly, tonelessly.

In his chair, Helmar said, "Go closer, Doctor. You'll see how he met his death."

Getting up, Parsons walked toward the wall. What at first appeared to be a small spot on the left breast of the man turned out to be something quite different. Here, beyond a doubt, was the cause of death. How out of place in this world, Parsons thought. He gazed up at it, amazed. But there was no doubt.

From the dead man's chest protruded the feathered, notched end of an arrow.

NINE

AT A SIGNAL from Loris, a servant approached Parsons. Bowing formally, the servant set down an object at Parsons' feet. He recognized it at once. Dented, stained, it was still familiar. His gray instrument case.

"We were not able to get you," Helmar said, "but we managed to pick this up. In the hotel lobby. During the confusion, after the government understood that the girl would recover."

With tension, they watched as he opened the instrument case and began inspecting the contents.

"We examined those instruments," Loris said, from over his shoulder. "But none of our technicians could make use of them. Our orientation does not equip us— we lack the basic principles. If you don't have all you need, we can supply you with other medical material which we dredged from the past. Originally, we imagined that if we had the material, we could make use of it ourselves."

Parsons said, "How long has this man been in the cube?"

"He has been dead thirty-five years," Loris said matter-of-factly.

Parsons said, "I'll know more once I've been able to examine him. Can he be brought out of the cold-pack?"

"Yes," Helmar said. "For no more than half an hour at a time, however."

"That should be enough," Parsons said.

Almost altogether, Helmar and Loris said, "Then you'll do it?"

"I'll try," he answered.

A wave of relief ran between the two of them; relaxing, they smiled at him. The tension in the room waned.

"Is there any reason," Parsons said, "why you can't tell me your relation to this man?" He faced Loris squarely.

After a pause, she said, "He's my father."

For a moment, the significance did not register. And then he thought, *But how can she know?*

Loris said, "I'd prefer not to tell you any more. At least not now. Later." She seemed tired out by the situation. "Let me have a servant show you to your apartment, and then perhaps we can—" She glanced at the man in the cube. "Perhaps you could begin your examination of him."

"I'd like to get some rest first," Parsons said. "After a good night's sleep I'd be in better shape."

Their disappointment showed clearly. But immediately Loris nodded, and then, more reluctantly, Helmar. "Of course," she said.

A servant came to show him to his apartment. Carrying Parsons' gray case, the servant preceded him up a wide flight of stairs. The man glanced back once, but said nothing. In silence they reached the apartment; the servant held the door open for Parsons, and he entered.

What luxury, he thought. Beyond doubt, he was the honored guest of the Lodge.

And with good reason!

At dinner that night he learned, from Loris and Helmar, the physical layout of their Lodge. They were slightly over twenty miles from the city which he had first encountered, the capital, at which the Soul Cube and Fountain were located. Here in the Lodge, Loris, as the Mother Superior, lived with her entourage. Like some great, opulent queen bee, Parsons thought. In this busy hive. Beyond that area controlled by the government; this was sacred land.

The Lodge, like a Roman demesne, was self-contained, independent economically and physically. Underneath the buildings were giant power turbines, atomic generators a century old. He had briefly glimpsed the subterranean landscape of drive-trains and whirring spheres, in some cases rust-covered masses of machines that still managed to roar and throb. But, as he had tried to penetrate further, he had been firmly turned back by armed uniformed guards, youths wearing the familiar Wolf emblem.

Food was grown artificially in subsurface chemical tanks. Clothing and furniture were processed from plastic raw materials by robots working somewhere on the grounds. Building materials, industrial supplies, everything that was needed, was manufactured and repaired on the Lodge grounds. A complete world, the core of which, like the city, was the cube. The miniature "soul" with which he would soon be working. He didn't have to be told how carefully the secret of its existence was kept. Probably only a few persons knew of it; probably not more than a fraction of those living and working at the Lodge. And how many of them understood its purpose, the reason for its existence? Perhaps only Loris and Helmar knew.

As they sat at the table, sipping after-dinner coffee and brandy, he asked Helmar bluntly, "Are you related to Loris?"

"Why do you ask?" Helmar said.

"You resemble the man in the cube—her father. And you resemble her, faintly."

Helmar shook his head. "No relation." His earlier excitement and eagerness now seemed masked over by politeness. And yet Parsons felt it still there, still smoldering.

There were so many things that Parsons did not understand. Too much, he decided, was being kept back. He had accepted the obvious: Loris and Helmar were acting illegally. Had been for some time. The very possession of the miniature cube was clearly a crime of the first magnitude. The maintenance of the body, the attempt to restore it to life—all were part of a painstakingly guarded and constructed plan of which the government and certainly the other tribes knew nothing.

He could understand Loris' desire to see her father alive. It was a natural emotion, common possible to all societies, including his own. He could understand the elaborate lengths she had gone to, in attempting to realize that wish. With her great influence and power, it might actually be possible to do this—as contrary as it was to everything the society stood for. After all, the man had been preserved uncorrupted for all of Loris' lifetime. The cube, the complex maintenance equipment, the whole Lodge itself, was geared to this task. The development and use of the time dredge, no doubt. If so much had already been done, the rest might follow.

But out of all this, one element still made no sense. In this society, all zygotes were developed and preserved by the Fountain, a purely artificial process.

Parsons chose his words carefully. "This man," he said to Loris. "Your father. Was he born at the Fountain?"

Both she and Helmar regarded him with equal caution. "No one is born outside the Fountain," Loris said in a low voice.

Helmar, with impatience, said, "What does such information have to do with your work? We have complete data on his physical condition at the time of his death. It's his death that's germane to you, not his birth."

"Who built the cube?" Parsons demanded bluntly.

"Why?" Loris said, almost inaudibly. She glanced at Helmar.

"The design," Helmar explained slowly, "is the same as the Fountain the government operates. No special knowledge was required to duplicate on a small scale what the government operates on a large scale."

"Somebody brought schematics here and constructed all this," Parsons persisted. "Obviously at great risk, and for considerable purpose."

Loris said, "To preserve *him*. My father."

At once, Parsons pounced; he felt his pulse race. "Then the cube was built *after* his death?

Neither of them answered.

"I don't see," Loris said finally, "what this has to do with your work. As Helmar says."

"I'm a hired employee, then?" Parsons said. "Not a genuine equal who can communicate with you as equals?"

Helmar glared at him, but Loris seemed more troubled than angry. Falteringly, she said, "No, not at all. It's just that the risk is so great. And it actually doesn't concern you, does it? Why should it, Doctor? When you treat a patient, a person who's sick or injured, do you inquire into his background, his beliefs, his purpose in life, his philosophy?"

"No," he admitted.

"We'll repay you," Loris said. "We can place you in any time period that you desire." Across the table from him, she smiled hopefully, coaxingly.

But Parsons said, "I have a wife whom I love. All I want to do is get back to her."

"That's so," Helmar said. "We noticed her while we were out scouting you."

"And knowing that," Parsons said, "you still brought me here, without my knowledge or permission. I gather that my personal feelings are of no concern to you." He hesitated. "In your estimation, I'm no better than a slave!"

"That's not true," Loris said. And he saw tears in her eyes. "You don't have to help us. You can go back to your own time if you want. It's your choice." Suddenly she rose from the table. "Excuse me," she said in a choked voice, and ran at once from the room.

Presently Helmar said, "You can sympathize with her feelings." He sat stoically sipping his coffee. "There's never been any chance before your coming. Let's acknowledge that you don't particularly care for me. But that's not the issue. You're not doing this for me. You're doing it for her."

The man had a point there.

And yet, even Loris had hung back, had not given

him honest answers. The whole atmosphere was pervaded with this sense of the hidden, the concealed. Why from him? If they trusted him enough to show him the man in the cube, to reveal the cube itself, then what more could there be? Did they suppose that if he knew more about them, he would not co-operate?

He filed his suspicions away, and sat, like Helmar, sipping his coffee royal. Inobtrusively, servants came and departed.

Neither he nor Helmar said anything; they sipped in silence. The brandy was very good, an authentic cognac. At last Helmar put down his cup and stood up.

"Ready, Doctor?" he said. "To make your initial exploratory examination?"

Parsons, too, stood. "Yes," he said. "Let's go."

TEN

THE THREE of them stood together, watching tensely as automatic machinery moved the cube forward, toward them. The cube came directly in front of them and stopped there.

The chamber was a blaze of lights. In the glare, Parsons watched the cube gradually tip backward until it came to rest. Within its depths the inert figure drifted quietly, eyes closed, body relaxed. The dead god, suspended between worlds, waiting to return . . .

And in the chamber, his people.

The chamber was crowded. Men who had stayed in the shadows until now were beginning to emerge. Parsons had not realized the extent of the project. He paused to take in the sight of this first appearance in real force, the actual strength that operated the Lodge.

Was it his imagination, or did they resemble one another? Of course, all members of this society had some similar characteristics, the same general skull formation and hair texture. And the clothing of this group was identical throughout, the gray robe and chest-emblem of the Wolf Tribe.

But there was more. The ruddy cast to the skin. A certain heaviness of the brow. Wide forehead. Flaring nostrils. As if they were of one family.

He counted forty men and sixteen women and then lost track. They were moving about, murmuring to one another. Taking places where they could watch him as he worked. They wanted to see every move he made.

Now the cube had been opened by Lodge technicians. The cold-pack was being sucked out greedily by plastic suction tendrils. In a moment the body would be exposed.

"These people shouldn't be here," Parsons said nervously. "I'll have to open his chest and plug in a pump. Danger of infection will be enormous."

The men and women heard him, but none of them budged.

"They feel they have a right to be here," Helmar said.

"But you people admittedly know nothing about medicine, about hygiene—"

"You worked on the girl Icara in public," Helmar said. "And you have numerous sterilizing agents in your case; we were able to identify them."

Parsons cursed under his breath. He turned away from Helmar and slid on his plastic protective gloves. Now he began arranging his instruments on a portable worktable. As the last of the cold-pack was drained off by the suction tendrils, Parsons flicked on a high-frequency field and placed the potentials on each side of the cube. The terminals hummed and glowed as the field warmed. Now the inert body was within a zone of bacteria-destroying radiation. He concentrated the field briefly on his instruments and gloves. The watching men and women took everything in without expression, faces blank with concentration.

Abruptly the cold-pack was gone. The body was exposed.

Parsons moved into activity. There had been no tangible decay. The body appeared perfectly fresh. He touched the lifeless wrist. It was *cold*. A chilling effluvium that trickled up his arm and made him quickly let go. The utter cold of outer space. He shivered and wondered how he was going to work.

"He will warm rapidly," Helmar grated. "It's no form of refrigeration you're familiar with. Molecular velocity has not been reduced. It has been differently phased."

The body was now warm enough to touch. Whatever alteration had been made in the vibrational pattern, the molecules were already beginning to return to their natural rate.

With scrupulous care, Parsons locked a mechanical lung in place and activated it. While the lung exerted rhythmic pressure on the immobile chest, he concentrated on the heart. He punctured the rib cage and plugged the Dixon pump into the vascular system, bypassing the suspended heart. The pump went immediately to work. Blood flowed. Both respiration and circulation resumed in this body that had died thirty-five years ago. Now, if there hadn't been much tissue deterioration from lack of oxygen and nutrition, especially in the brain . . .

Unnoticed, Loris had come over beside him, so that now her body pressed against him. Rigid as stone, she peered down.

"Instead of removing the arrow from the heart," Parsons said, "I have gone around the heart. Temporarily, at least." Now he inspected the injured organ itself.

The arrow had penetrated accurately. Probably there was little he could do to restore the organ. But, with the proper tool, he plucked the arrow out and tossed it to the floor. Blood oozed.

"It can be repaired," he said to Loris. "But the big question has to do with brain damage. If it's too great, I recommend that we destroy him." The alternative, letting him live, would not be pleasant.

"I see," she said in a stricken voice. No more than a whisper.

"In my opinion," Parsons said, addressing both her and the group, "we should proceed now."

"You mean try to revive him?" she said. He had to catch hold of her; she had begun to sway, and he saw that her eyes were almost blind with fear.

"Yes," he said. "May I?"

"Suppose you fail," she whispered, appealing to him. "I have as much chance of success as I will ever have," he said frankly. "Every time he's revived, there will be some further deterioration of brain tissue."

"Then go ahead," she said in a stronger voice.

Helmar, behind them, said, "And don't fail." He did not say it as a threat; his voice had more a patently fanatical tone. As if, to him, failure simply could not occur; it was not possible.

Parsons said, "With the pump operating, he should revive very shortly." With instruments, he listened for pulse, for the man's breathing. That is, if he ever does, he thought to himself.

The man stirred. His eyelids fluttered.

A gasp came from the watchers. A simultaneous expression of amazement and joy.

"He is living by use of the mechanical pump," Parsons said to Loris. "Of course, if everything goes well—"

"Ultimately you will stitch the heart fiber and attempt to remove the pump," Loris finished.

"Yes," he said.

Loris said, "Doctor, would you please do that now? There are conditions that you know nothing about; please believe me when I say that if there's any possibility that you could perform the surgery on the heart at this time . . ." Pleadingly, she caught hold of his hands; he felt her strong fingers dig into his flesh. Gazing up at him she said, "For my sake. Even if there's more risk this way, I feel convinced that you should go ahead. I have good reasons. Please, Dr. Parsons."

Reluctantly, studying the pulse and respiration of the patient, he said, "He will have to mend over a period of weeks. You understand that. He can't take any strain, of any sort, until the fiber—"

"You'll do it?" she said, her eyes shining.

Assembling his instruments, he began the grueling task of repairing the ruptured heart.

When he had finished, he discovered that only Loris remained in the chamber; the others had been sent out, undoubtedly on her order. She sat silently across from him, her arms folded. Now she seemed more composed. But her face still had the rigidity, the fear.

"All right?" she said with a tremor.

"Evidently," he said. Exhausted, he started putting away his instruments.

"Doctor," she breathed, rising and approaching him, "you have done a profound thing. Not only for us, but for the world."

Too worn-out to pay much attention to her, he stripped off his gloves. "I'm sorry," he said. "I'm too tired to talk. I'd like to go up to my apartment and go to bed."

"You'll be on call? If anything goes wrong?" As he started from the chamber, Loris hurried after him. "What should we watch for? We'll have attendants on hand at all times, of course . . . I realize that he's quite feeble, and will be for some time." Now she made him halt. "When will he be conscious?"

"Probably in an hour," he said, at the door.

That apparently satisfied her. Nodding in a preoccupied fashion, she started back to the patient.

By himself, he ascended the stairs, and, after getting the wrong room several times, at last managed to find his own apartment. Inside, he shut and locked the door and sank down on the bed to rest. He felt too weary to undress or get under the covers.

The next he knew, the door was open. Loris stood in the entrance, gazing down at him. The room had become dark—or had he lain down with the light off? Groggily, he started to sit up.

"I thought you might want something to eat," she said. "It's after midnight." As she switched on a lamp and went over to pull the drapes, he saw that a servant had followed her into the apartment.

"Thanks," he said, rubbing his eyes.

Loris dismissed the servant and began lifting the pewter covers from the dishes. He could smell the warm, rich odors of food.

"Any change in your father?" he asked.

Loris said, "He became conscious for a moment. At least, he opened his eyes. And I had a distinct impression that he was aware of me. And then he went to sleep; he's sleeping now."

"He'll sleep a lot," Parsons said. But he thought, That may indicate possible brain damage.

She had arranged two chairs at a small table, and now she let him seat her. "Thank you," she said. "You put everything you had into what you did. Such an impressive spectacle for us to see—a doctor and his devotion to healing." She smiled at him; in the half-light of the room her lips were full and moist. Since he had last seen her she had changed to a different dress, and her hair, now, was tied back, held in place by a clasp. "You're a very good man," she said. "A very kind and worthy man. We're ennobled by your presence."

Embarrassed, he shrugged, not knowing what to say.

"I'm sorry to make you uncomfortable," she said. She began to eat, and he did so too. But after a few bites he realized that he was not hungry. Feeling restless, he got to his feet, excusing himself. Walking to the veranda of the apartment he opened the glass door and stepped outside, into the cold night air.

Luminous night moths fluttered beyond the railing, among the trees and moist branches. Somewhere in the forest small animals crashed about, growled, moved sullenly off. Sounds of breaking twigs, stealthy footpads. Hissing.

"Cats," Loris whispered. "Domestic cats." She had come out, too, to stand beside him in the darkness.

"Gone wild?"

She turned toward him. "You know, Doctor, there is a basic fallacy in their thinking."

"Who do you mean by 'they'?"

Waving her hand vaguely she said, "The government. The whole system, here. The Soul Cube, the Lists. That girl, Icara. The one you saved." Her voice became firm. "She killed herself because she had been disfigured. She knew she'd drag down the tribe when List time came. She knew she'd score badly because of her physical appearance. *But such things aren't inherited!*" Bitterness swept through her voice. "She sacrificed herself for nothing. Who gained? What good did her death do? She was certain it was for the benefit of the tribe—for the race. I've seen enough of death."

He knew, hearing her, that she was thinking about her father. "Loris," he said. "If you can go back into the past, why didn't you try to change it? Prevent his death?"

"You don't know what we know," she said. "The possibility of changing the past is limited. It's very hard." She sighed. "Don't you suppose we tried?" Her voice rose now. "Don't you think we went back again and again, trying to make it come out differently? And it never did."

"The past is immutable?" he said.

"We don't understand it quite. Some things can be changed. But not this. Not the thing that matters! There's some kind of central force that eludes us. Some power working . . ."

"You really love him," he said, moved by her emotion.

She nodded faintly. Now he saw her hand lift; she wiped at her eyes. Dimly, he could make out her face, her trembling lips, long lashes, the great black eyes sparkling with tears.

"I'm sorry," Parsons said. "I didn't mean to—"

"It's all right. We've been under so much strain. For so long. You understand, I've never seen him alive. And, to look at him day after day, suspended in there, beyond reach—utterly remote from us. All the time, when I was a child, growing up, I thought of nothing else. To bring him back. To have him again, to possess him. If he could be made to live again—" Her hands opened, reached out, yearning, groping, closing again on nothing. "And now that we do have him back—" Abruptly, she broke off.

"Go on," Parsons prompted.

Loris shook her head and turned away. Parsons touched her soft black hair, moist with the night mist. She did not protest. He drew her close to him; still she did not protest. Her warm breath drifted up in a cloud, rising around him, mixing with the sweet scent of her hair. Against him her body vibrated, intense and burning with suppressed emotion. Her bosom rose and fell, outlined against the starlight, her body trembling under the silk of her robe.

His hand touched her cheek, then her throat. Her full lips were close to him. Her eyes were half-closed, head bent back, breath coming rapidly. "Loris," he said softly.

She shook her head. "No. Please, no."

"Why don't you trust me? Why don't you want to tell me? What is there you can't—"

With a convulsive moan she broke away and ran toward the doorway, robes fluttering after her.

Catching up with her, he put his arms around her, holding her from escaping. "What's the matter?" he said, trying to see her, trying to read the expression on her face. Wanting to make her look at him.

"I—" she began.

The door to the apartment flew open. Helmar, his face distorted, said, "Loris. He—" Seeing Parsons he said, "Doctor. Come."

They ran, the three of them, down the corridor to the stairs, down the stairs; gasping, they reached the room in which Loris' father lay. Attendants ushered them in. Parsons caught sight of elaborate equipment, unfamiliar to him, in the process of being assembled.

On the bed lay Loris' father, his lips parted, his eyes glazed. His eyes, sightless in death, stared up at the ceiling.

"Cold-pack," Loris was saying, somewhere in the background, as Parsons grabbed out his instruments.

Lifting aside the sheet, Parsons saw the feathered, notched end of an arrow protruding from the dead man's chest.

"Again," Helmar said, in a tone of absolute hopelessness. "We thought . . ." His voice trailed off, baffled and wretched. "Get the pack around him?" he shouted suddenly, and attendants pushed between Parsons and the bed. He saw them expertly lift the corpse and slide it into the vacant cube; cold-pack poured in and surrounded the form until it became blurred and obscured.

After a time Loris said bitterly, "Well, we were right." The fury in her voice shocked Parsons; he turned involuntarily, and saw an expression he had never before witnessed on a woman's face. A complete and absolute hate.

"Right about what?" he managed to ask.

Lifting her head, she gazed at him; her eyes seemed to have shrunk so that the pupils gleamed like tiny, burning points, no longer located in space but somehow hovering before him, blinding him almost. "Someone is working against us," she said. "They have it, too. Control of time. Thwarting us, enjoying it . . ." She laughed. "Yes, *enjoying* it. Mocking us." Abruptly, with a swing of her robes, she turned away from Parsons and disappeared past the ring of attendants.

Parsons, stepping back, saw the final surface of the Soul Cube slide into place. Once again the figure floated in eternal stasis. Dead and silent. Beyond the reach of the living.

ELEVEN

STANDING beside Parsons, Helmar muttered, "It's not your fault." Together, they watched the cube being lifted upright. "We have enemies," Helmar said. "This happened before, when we went back into time and tried to recreate the situation. But we thought it was a natural force, a phenomenon of time. Now we know better. Our worst fears are justified. This did not happen through an impersonal force."

"Perhaps not," Parsons said. "But don't see motive where there is none." *They are a little paranoid,* he decided. *Possibly rightly so.* "As Loris told me," he continued, "none of you fully comprehend the principles that lie behind time. Isn't it still possible that—"

"No," Helmar said flatly. "I know. We all know." He started to speak further, and then, seeing something, he stopped.

Parsons turned. He, too, had meant to go on, but his words choked off.

For the first time he had noticed her.

She had entered silently, a few moments ago. Two armed guards stood on each side of her. A stir went through the room, among the people present.

She was old. The first old person that Parsons had seen in this world.

Approaching the old woman, Loris said, "He is dead again. They managed to destroy him once again."

The old woman advanced silently toward the cube,

toward the dead man who lay within. She was, even at her age, strikingly handsome. Tall and dignified. A mane of white hair down the back of her neck . . . the same broad forehead. Heavy brows. Strong nose and chin. Stern, powerful face.

The same as the others. This old woman, the man in the cube, everybody at the Lodge—all partook of the same physical characteristics.

The stately old woman had reached the rim of the cube. She gazed at it, unspeaking.

Loris took her arm. "Mother—"

There it was. The old woman was Loris' mother. The wife of the man in the cube.

It fitted. He had been in the cube thirty-five years. The old woman was probably seventy. *His wife!* This pair, this couple, had spawned the powerful, full-breasted creature who ruled the Wolf Tribe, the most potent human being alive.

"Mother," Loris said. "We'll try once more. I promise."

Now the old woman had noticed Parsons. Instantly, her face became fierce. "Who are you?" she asked in a deep, vibrant voice.

Loris said, "He's the doctor who tried to bring Corith back."

The old woman was still looking frigidly at Parsons. Gradually her features softened. "It's not your fault," she said at last. For a moment she lingered by the cube. "Later," she said. "Once more." She turned for a last look at Parsons, then at the man in the cube. And then the old woman and her attendants moved away, back toward the lift from which they had emerged. She had come up from the subsurface levels that honeycombed the ground beneath their feet—unguessed regions that he had never seen and probably would never see. The guarded, secret core of the Lodge.

All the men and women stood silently as the old woman passed among them. Heads bowed slightly. Reverence. They were all acknowledging her, Loris' mother. The regal, white-haired old woman who moved slowly and calmly across the room, away from the cube. Her face creased and frozen in grief. The mother of the Mother Superior—

The mother of them all!

At the lift she halted and half-turned. She made a faint motion with her hand, a motion that took them all in. She was recognizing them. Her children.

It was clear. Helmar, Loris, all the rest of them, all seventy or so, were descended from this old lady, and from the man who lay in the cube. Yet one thing did not fit.

The man in the cube and this old woman. If they were man and wife—

"I'm glad you saw her," Loris said, from beside him.

"Yes," he said.

"Did you see how she took it? She was an inspiration to us, in our deprivation. A model for us to follow." Now Loris, too, seemed to have regained her poise.

"Good," Parsons murmured. His mind was racing. *The old woman and the man in the cube.* Corith, she had called him. Corith—her father. That made sense. Everything made sense but one thing. And that one thing was a little difficult to get past.

Both Corith and the old woman, his wife, showed identical physical characteristics.

"What is it?" Loris was demanding. "What's wrong?"

Parsons shook himself and forced his mind to turn outward. "I'm having trouble," he said. "To have him die again, and in the same way."

"Always," Loris said. "It's always the same way. The arrow driven through his heart, killing him instantly."

"No variation?"

"None of importance."

He said, "When did it happen?" His question did not seem to be clear to her. "The arrow," he said. "There are no such weapons in use in this time period, are there? I assume it happened in the past."

"True," she admitted with a shake of her head. "Our work with time, our explorations—"

"Then you had the time-travel equipment first," he said. "Before his death."

She nodded.

Parsons said, "At least thirty-five years ago. Before your birth."

"We have been at it a long time."

Why? What are you trying to do? He shot the question at her, forcing it on her. "What's this scheme you all have? Tell me. If you expect me to help you—"

"We don't expect you to help us," she said bitterly. "There's nothing you can do for us. We'll send you back. Your efforts are over; you have no further job here." Leaving him, she moved away, her head bowed, lost in contemplation of the disaster that had befallen them all.

The whole family. Parsons thought as he watched her thread her way among the others. Brothers and sisters. But that still did not explain the physical resemblance between Corith and his wife; the thing had to be carried back to another level.

And then he saw something that made him shrink into immobility. This time, he was the only one who had seen. The others were too wrapped up in their problems. Even Loris hadn't noticed.

Here was the missing element. The basic key that had been lacking.

She was standing in the shadows at the very edge of the room. Out of sight. She had come up with the other old woman, Loris' mother. But she had not emerged from the darkness. She remained hidden, watching everything that happened from her place of concealment.

She was unbelievably old. A tiny shriveled-up thing. Wizened and bent, claw-like hands, broomstick legs beneath the hem of her dark robe. A dry little bird face, wrinkled skin, like parchment. Two dulled eyes, set deep in the yellowing skull, a wisp of white hair like a spider web.

"She's completely deaf," Helmar said softly, close by him. "And almost blind."

Parsons started. *"Who is she?"*

"She's almost a century old. She was the first. The very first." Helmar's voice broke with emotion. He was shaking visibly, in the possession of primordial tidal surges that vibrated through his entire body. "Nixina—the mother of them both. The mother of Corith and Jepthe. She is the *Urmutter*."

"Corith and Jepthe are brother and sister?" Parsons demanded.

Helmar nodded. "Yes. We're all related."

His mind spun wildly. Inbreeding. But why? And in this society, how?

How was inbreeding accomplished in a world where the racial stock was thrown into one common pool? How had this magnificent family, this genuine family, been maintained?

Three generations. The grandmother, the mother and father. Now the children.

Helmar had said: *She was the first.* The tiny shriveled-up creature was the first—*what?*

Now the frail shape moved forward. The eyes lost their dulled film, and Parsons saw that she was looking directly at him. The shrunken lips trembled, and then, in a voice audible to him, she said, "Do I see a white person over there?" Step by step, as if blown gradually forward by some invisible wind, she approached him. Helmar at once hurried to her side, to assist her.

Holding out her hand to Parsons, the old woman said, "Welcome." He found himself taking the hand; it felt dry and cold and rough. "You're the—what is the word?" For a moment the alertness faded from the eyes. And then it returned. "The doctor who tried to bring my son back to life." The old woman paused, her breath coming irregularly. "Thank you for your efforts," she finished in a hoarse whisper.

Not certain what to reply, Parsons said, "I'm sorry it wasn't successful."

"Perhaps . . ." Her voice ebbed, like the rise and fall of a far-off sea. "The next time." She smiled vaguely. And then, as before, her faculties focused; the brightness returned. "Isn't it an irony, that a white person would be involved in this . . . or haven't they told you what we are trying to do?"

The whole room had become silent. All eyes had become fixed on Parsons and the ancient little woman.

No one spoke; no one dared try to hinder her. Parsons, too, felt some of their veneration.

He said, "No. No one has told me."

"You should know," Nixina said. "It's not just unless you know. I'll tell you. My son Corith is responsible for the idea. Many years ago, when he was a young man like yourself. He was very brilliant. And so ambitious. He wanted to make everything right, erase the Terrible Five Hundred Years . . ."

Parsons recognized the term. The period of white supremacy. He found himself nodding.

"You saw the portraits?" the old woman breathed, gazing past Parsons. "Hanging in the central hall . . . the great men in their ruffled collars. The noble explorers." She chuckled, a dry laugh, like leaves blowing in the wind. Dried-up, fallen leaves of nightfall. "Corith wanted to go back. And the government knew how to go back, but it didn't realize that it knew."

Still no one spoke. No one tried to stop her. It was impossible; they could not presume.

Nixina said, "So my son went back. To the first New England. Not the famous one, but the other one. The real one. In California. Nobody remembers . . . but Corith read all the records, the old books." Again she chuckled. "He wanted to start there, in Nova Albion. But he didn't get very far." The dulled eyes blazed. Like Loris', Parsons thought. For a moment he caught the heritage, the resemblance. Bending, he listened to the dry whisper as it went on, only half directed to him, more a kind of remembering rather than any communication. "On June 17," she said. "In 1579. He sailed into a port to work on his ship. He claimed the land for the Queen. How well we all know." She turned to Helmar.

"Yes," Helmar agreed quietly.

"For a little more than a month," the old woman said. "He was there. They careened their ship."

Parsons said, "The *Golden Hind*." He understood now.

"And Corith came down," the old woman whispered, smiling up at Parsons. "And instead . . . they shot him. Through his heart, with an arrow. And he died." Her eyes faded, and then became opaque.

"She'd better rest," Helmar said. Gently, he led the old woman away; the other gray-clad shapes closed in, and she was gone. Parsons no longer saw her.

That was their great plan. To change the past by going back centuries, before the time of the white empires. To find Drake encamped in California, helpless while his ship was being repaired. To kill him, the first Englishman to claim part of the New World for England.

They had special hatred for the English; of all the colonial powers, the English had been the most conscious of race. The most certain of their superiority to the Indians. They had not interbred.

Parsons thought, They wanted to be there, on the shore, to meet the English. Waiting. To shoot them down with equal weapons, or possibly even superior weapons. To make it a fair contest—or an unfair contest, but the other way.

How could he blame them? They had come back, centuries later, regrouped, to regain control of their own lives. But the memory had not died. Revenge. To avenge the crimes of the past.

But Drake—or somebody at the time of Drake—had shot first.

By himself, Parsons found his way to the central hall in which the portraits of the sixteenth century explorers hung. For a time he studied them. One after another, he thought. Drake would have been first, and then— Cortez? Pizarro? And so on, down the line. As they landed with their helmeted troops, they would be wiped out—the conquerors, the plunderers and the pirates. Prepared to find a passive, helpless population, they would instead come face-to-face with the calculating, advanced descendents of that population. Grim and ready. Waiting.

There certainly was justice to it. Harsh, cruel. But he could not hold back his tacit sympathy.

Returning to the portrait of Drake, he scrutinized it more closely. The sharp, well-trimmed beard. High forehead. Wrinkles at the outer corners of the eyes. The well-chiseled nose. The Englishman's hand attracted Parsons' attention. Tapered, elongated fingers, almost feminine. The hand of a sailor? More the man of noblemen. An aristocrat. Of course, the portrait was idealized.

Going on, he found a second portrait, this one an engraving. This one showed Drake's hair as curly. And the eyes much larger and deeper colored. Rather fleshy cheeks. A less expertly done portrait, but perhaps more accurate. And in this one, the hands small and even weak looking. The hands of a ship's captain?

Something about the portrait struck him as familiar. Lines of the face. The curly hair. The eyes.

For a long time he studied the portrait, but he could not pin down the familiarity. At last, reluctantly, he gave up.

He hunted throughout the Lodge until he managed to locate Helmar. He found him conferring with several of his brethern, but at sight of Parsons, Helmar broke off.

Parsons said, "I'd like to see something."

"Of course," Helmar said formally.

"The arrow that I removed from Corith's chest."

"It has been taken below," Helmar said. "I can have it brought up, if you feel it's important."

"Thanks." Parsons said. He waited tensely while two servants were sent off. "Have you given it a thorough examination?" he asked Helmar.

"For what?"

He did not answer. At last the arrow, in a transparent bag, was brought to him. Eagerly, he unfastened the wrapping and seated himself to study the thing.

"Could I have my instrument case?" he asked presently.

The servants were dispatched; they soon returned with the dented gray case. Opening it, Parsons lifted out various tools; before long he had begun cutting microscopic sections from the wood of the arrow, and then the feathers, and, at last, the flint point. Using chemicals from his supply, he arranged first one test and then another. Helmar watched. After a time Loris appeared, evidently summoned.

"What are you looking for?" Loris asked, her face still strained.

Parsons said, "I want this flint analyzed. But I can't do it."

"I suppose we have the equipment to do it," Helmar said. "But it would take up quite a time to get the results."

Slightly more than an hour later, the results were brought to him. He read the report, and then passed it on to Loris and Helmar.

Parsons said, "The feathers are artificial. A thermoplastic. The wood is yew. The head is flint, but chipped with a metal tool, such as a chisel."

They stared at him in bewilderment. "But we saw him die," Loris said. "Back in the past—in 1579. In Nova Albion."

"*Who* shot him?" Parsons said.

"We never saw. He started down the cliff and then he fell.

"This arrow," Parsons said, "was not produced by New World Indians of the sixteenth century or by anyone of that century. It was made later than 1930, considering the substance from which the feathers were made."

Corith had not been killed by someone from the past!

TWELVE

IT WAS evening. Jim Parsons and Loris were standing on the balcony of the Lodge, watching the distant lights of the city. The lights shifted and moved constantly. An ever-changing pattern that glittered and winked through the clear darkness of the night. Like man-made stars, Parsons thought. And all colores.

"In that city," Loris said. "Somebody there. Some person down among those lights made that arrow and shot it into my father's chest. And the second arrow, too. The one that still is buried in him."

And, Parsons thought, whoever it is has machinery for moving into time. Unless these people are misleading me. How do I know Corith died in Nova Albion, in 1579? He could have been shot down here, and the story could have been a concoction, put together by these people. But then, why would they have gone to the trouble to summon a doctor from the past? To heal a man whom they themselves had murdered?

"If you went back two times," he said aloud, "after he was shot originally, why didn't you see his attacker? Arrows don't carry far."

"It's quite rocky," Loris said. "Cliffs all along the beach. And my father—" She hesitated. "He kept himself apart, even from us. We were directly above the *Golden Hind*, looking down on Drake and his men while they worked."

"They didn't see you?"

"We put on clothing of the period. Fur wrappers. And they were busy working on their little ship. Working very industriously."

He said, "An arrow. Not a musket shot."

"We could never account for that," Loris said. "But Drake was not on the ship. He and a group of his men had gone off; that made by father's task more difficult. He had to wait. And then Drake appeared down the beach a distance, and held some sort of conference. So my father hurried down that way, out of our immediate sight."

"What would Corith have killed Drake with?"

"A force tube, like this." She went to her room and returned to the balcony, carrying a weapon familiar to Parsons. The *shupos* had had them, and so had Stenog. Evidently this was the standard hand weapon of this period.

"What would his crew have thought? They knew what weapons the Indians had."

Loris said, "The more mysterious it was to Drake's crew, the better. All we cared about was getting at Drake. And making sure that they should know that Drake died at the hands of a red man."

"But would they know?"

"My father had made certain that they would know him to be an Indian. He worked for months on his disguise. At least, so my mother and grandmother tell me. I, of course, was not born yet. He had a special workroom down below, with all sorts of tools and materials. He kept his preparations secret, even from his mother and wife. From everyone. In fact"—her brow wrinkled with uneasiness as she remembered—"he didn't put on his costume until he was back at Nova Albion, out of the time ship and away from them. He claimed it was dangerous to let even his family see him in advance."

"Why?" Parsons said.

"He didn't trust anyone. Not even Nixina. Or so they say. Doesn't that seem odd to you? Surely he must have trusted them; he must have trusted his mother. But—" Awkwardly, she went on, her brow furrowed. "Anyhow, he worked by himself down below, telling nobody anything. He's supposed to have gotten incoherent with rage if anybody asked him questions. And Jepthe says he several times accused her of trying to spy on him. He was sure that someone was watching him at work, trying to gain entrance into his workroom for some evil purpose. So of course he kept it locked; he even locked himself in while he worked. I know he believed that almost everyone was against him, especially the servants. He refused to have any."

The man had been virtually a paranoid, Parsons thought. But it would fit with the grand scheme, the sense of heroic injustice and hate. How close the idealist, with his fanatical passion, was to the mentally disturbed.

"Anyhow," Loris said, "he intended finally to display himself. To be quite conspicuous as he killed Drake. So the crew would carry report back to Elizabeth that the red men had weapons superior to the English."

To him, the logic was fuzzy. And yet, what did it matter? Details did not concern them; the overall scheme, dazzling them, led them on, not such picayune matters as the incongruity of a twenty-fifth century hand weapon used in the sixteenth century. And certainly the English would be impressed.

"Why can't you continue without Corith?" he said.

Loris said, "Because you know only one part of our program."

"And what's the other part?"

"Do you want to know? Does it matter?"

He said, "Tell me."

Beside him, the woman sighed, shivering in the night air. "I want to go in," she said. "The darkness . . . it depresses me. All right?"

Together, they left the balcony and entered Loris' apartment.

This was the first time that Parsons had been invited here. At the threshold he paused. Through a half-opened closet door he made out the indistinct shapes of a woman's clothing. Robes and gowns. Slippers. And, on the far side of the room, satin covers on the wide bed. Lush wine-colored drapes. Thick multi-colored carpet which he knew at once had been pilfered from the Middle Eastern past. Someone had used the time dredge to its best advantage, furnishing the apartment in excellent taste.

Loris seated herself in an easy chair, and Parsons came up close behind her and put his hands on her warm, smooth shoulders. "Tell me the part I don't know," he said. "About your father."

Loris, her back to him, said, "You know that all the males are sterile." She raised her head, shaking her mane of black hair aside. "And you know that Corith is not. Otherwise, how could I exist?"

"True," he said.

"Nixina, my grandmother, was the Mother Superior at her time, decades ago. She managed to get him past the sterilization procedures; it was almost impossible because they're so careful. But she was able to, and in the records he was listed as sterilized. Under his hands her body trembled. "The women are not, as you know. So there was no difficulty in his mating with my mother, Jepthe. The union took place here, in secret. Then the zygote was taken, in cold-pack, to the great central Fountain and placed in the Soul Cube. Jepthe was the Mother Superior at that time, you understand. She kept the zygote separate until it had developed into a fetus . . . in fact, all along its trip to full embryo and at last birth."

"And this was done with the rest of your family?"

"Yes. My brother, Helmar. But—" Now she got up from the chair and moved away from him. "You see, they managed to sterilize all the males who came after Corith. He was the only one who escaped." Now she was silent.

Parsons said, "Then for further reproduction of your family, you're dependent on Corith."

The woman nodded.

"Including your own. If you choose to continue."

"Yes," she said. "But that's not important now."

"Why was it ever important? What did you mean to do with this family?"

Raising her head she confronted him proudly. "We're not like the others, Doctor. Nixina tells us that she's a full-blooded Iroquois Indian. We're practically pure. Couldn't you see?" She put her hand to her cheek. "Look at my face. My skin. Don't you think it's true?"

"Possibly," he said. "It would be almost impossible to verify, though. Such a claim as that—it sounds more mystical than practical."

"I prefer to believe it," she said. "Certainly it's spiritually true. We are the spiritual heirs, their blood brothers in any and all meaningful senses. Even it it's only a myth."

Parsons reached out and touched her jaw, the firm boneline. She did not move back or protest.

"What we are going to do," she said, her face close to his, her breath stirring against his mouth, "is as follows. We intended to preempt your ancestors, Doctor. Unfortunately, it didn't work out. But if we had been successful, if we had been able to assassinate the white adventurers and pirates who came to the New World and established footholds, we would have installed our own stock—ourselves! What do you think of that?" A taunting smile appeared on her lips.

"Are you serious?" he said.

"Of course."

"You would have been the vanguard of civilization, then. Instead of the Elizabethans and Spanish gentry and Dutch traders."

Now, with deep seriousness, she said, "And it would not have been masters over slaves. The supremacy of one race over another. It would have been a natural relationship: *the future guiding the past.*"

He thought, Yes, it would have been more humane. No tribes to be wiped out, no concentration camps— euphemistically referred to as "reservations." Too bad, he thought. He felt real regret.

"You're sorry," she said, peering at him. "And you're white. How odd." It seemed to disconcert her. "You don't identify with those conquerors, do you?

And yet they built your civilization. We plucked you from the latter part of that world."

Parsons said, "I didn't burn witches, either. I have no sense of identification with many of those things. Are all whites alike?"

"No," she said. But she had become colder, now. The friendliness was gone. From beneath his hands she slipped away; all at once she had left him and was walking off.

Following her, he took hold of her, turned her toward him, and kissed her. Her eyes, dark and full, were fixed on him. But she did not try to draw away.

"You were protesting," she said, when he released her, "that we had kidnapped you away from your wife." She said it with hostility.

It was hard for him to defend himself. So he said nothing.

"Well," she said, "it's absurd anyhow. You'll be going back, wife or not."

"And you're full-blooded Indian and I'm white," he added ironically.

She said in a quiet voice, "Don't vilify me, Doctor. I'm not a fanatic. We're not contemptuous of you."

"Do you see me as a person?"

"Oh, you definitely bleed when cut," she said, laughing now but with no unkindness. At that, he had to smile too. Suddenly she threw her arms around him and hugged him with amazing vitality. "Well, Doctor," she said, "do you want to be my lover? Make up your mind."

Tightly, he said, "Remember, I'm not sterile."

"That's no problem for me. I'm the Mother Superior. I have access to every part of the Fountain. We have our regular procedure; if I become pregnant I can introduce the zygote into the Soul Cube, and"—she made a gesture of resignation—"plop. Lost forever, into the race."

He said, "All right, then."

At once she tore herself away from him. "Who said you could be my lover? Did I give you permission? I was just curious." She retreated from him, her lovely face alive with glee. "You don't want a fat squaw, any-how."

Moving quickly, he caught her. "Yes, I do," he said.

Later, as they lay together in the darkness, Loris whispered, "Is there anything else you want?"

Parsons had lit a cigarette. Smoking, meditating, he said, "Yes, there is."

Beside him, the woman rolled closer; pressing against him she said, "What is it?"

"I want to go back to see his death," he said.

"My father? Back to Nova Albion?" She sat up, brushing her long, untied hair back from her face.

"I want to be there," he said calmly.

In the dark he could feel her staring at him. And he could hear her breathing, the long, unsteady inhalations and then the rush with which she breathed out. "We weren't planning to try again," she murmured. Now she slid from the bed, and, in the gloom, padded barefoot in search of her robe. Outlined against the faint light from the window, she stood buttoning her robe around her and tying the sash.

"Let's try," he said.

She did not answer. But he knew, intuitively and with certitude, that they would.

Toward morning, as the first insipid gray appeared outside, filtering into the apartment through the drapes, he and Loris sat facing each other across a small glass-topped table on which were a stainless steel coffeepot, china cups and saucers, an overflowing ash tray. Her face fatigued, but still strong and vital, Loris said:

"You know, your willingness to do this—your desire to do this—makes me wonder about our whole plan." Smoke drifted from her lips, she set her cigarette down and began rubbing her throat. "I wonder if we're right. It's a little late to wonder that, isn't it?"

"A paradox," he said.

"Yes," she said. "We can only eradicate the whites by prevailing on a white to help us. But we recognized that when we first began scouting you."

"But at that time," he said, "you were making use of

my special talent. Now—" What was it now? He thought, More the whole person. Myself as an individual, not as a doctor. The person, not the skill. Because I am doing this knowingly. Deliberately. With full awareness of what the issues are.

This is my choice.

"Let me ask you something," he said. "Suppose you are successful. Won't that alter history? Won't Drake's death wipe out all of us, as products of a process that includes Drake? You, me, every one of us."

Loris said, "You must understand that we are not ignorant of these massive paradoxes. Since my father's time there has been continual experimentation with the results of altering the past, seeing exactly how the historic process proceeds after a change—even a minute one—has been made. There is a general tendency for the vast, inertial flow to rectify itself. To seek a sort of level. It's almost impossible to affect the far future. Like rocks thrown in a river . . . a series of ripples that finally die. To do what we want, we must manage to assassinate fifteen or sixteen major historic figures. Even so, we do not end European civilization. We do not fundamentally alter it. There will still be telephones and motorcars and Voltaire—we presume."

"But you're not sure."

"How could we be? We have reason to believe that, generally, the same persons who now exist will exist after our plan works out. Their condition, their status, will be different. Looking backward, the conditions become more affected the closer you get to the original moment. The sixteenth century will be completely different. The seventeenth, not completely but very much so. The eighteenth, different but recognizable. Or so we hypostatize. We could be wrong. There's much guesswork in this maneuvering with history. But—" Her voice became firm. "We've been back many times, and so far we've been able to make no changes whatsoever. Our problem is not that we risk altering the present, but that we've been unable to alter anything at all."

"It's possible," Parsons said, "that it can't be altered.

That the paradox obviates any meddling with the past—by definition."

"That may be. But we want to try." She pointed a coppery, tapered finger at him. "You must carry your paradox to its logical conclusion. If we obviate ourselves by succeeding in the past, then the agent that alters the past will have ceased to exist; hence, no alteration will have occurred. The worst that can happen is that we will wind up where we are now; unable to budge what has already occurred."

He had to admit that their reasoning was sound.

There was simply no complete theory about time, he realized. No hypothesis by which results could be anticipated.

Only experiment—and guesswork.

But, he thought, billions of human lives, complete civilizations, depend on how accurately these people have guessed. Wouldn't it be better not to risk further attempts to tamper? Shouldn't I, for the sake of centuries of human achievement and suffering, stay away from Nova Albion and 1579?

He had a theory, however. A theory that had entered his mind when he saw the plastic feathers of the arrow.

In fact, a theory that had come to mind when he had noticed something familiar in the engraving of Sir Francis Drake.

All the tampering had already been done. That was his theory. And, by going back, he would simply observe, not alter. The past had been tampered with up to the hilt, but none of them, not Loris, not even Corith, had recognized it.

The portrait of Drake, with the skin darkened, the beard and mustache removed, would have looked very much like a portrait of Al Stenog.

THIRTEEN

IN THE wheel chair, the ancient, tattered figure sat huddled in a heavy wool blanket. At first Nixina did not seem aware of him. She stood by the doorway, waiting. Then, at last, the eyes opened. Up from the depths swam a fragment of personality; he saw the consciousness there, in the expression. The coming to the surface, from sleep. For her, at her age, sleep was perpetual and natural; it ended only at unusual moments. And, before long, it would never end.

"Madam," he said.

Beside him, an armed attendant said, "Remember, she is deaf. Go closer and she'll be able to read your lips."

He did so.

"So you're going to try again," Nixina said, her voice a dry, rasping whisper.

"Yes," he said.

"Did you know," she whispered, "that I was along the other times?"

He could hardly believe it. Surely the strain—

"I intend to come this time," she told him. "It's my son, you recall." Her voice gained sudden vigor. "Don't you think if anyone can protect him, I can?"

There was nothing he could say to that.

"Helmar built me a special chair," she said, and in her tone he heard something that told him a great deal. He heard authority.

She had not always been old. Once she had been young, not blind and not deaf, and not infirm. This woman kept the rest of them going. She did not—and would never—permit them to stop. As long as she lived, she would keep them at her task. As she had kept her son at the task, until the moment of his death.

Now her voice sank back to the labored whisper. "So," she went on, "I'll be perfectly safe. I don't intend to interfere with what you're going to do." Plaintively, she asked, "Do you mind . . . can you tell me what you think you can do? They say you have a notion that you might do some good."

"I hope so," he said. "But I don't know." He became silent, then. There was nothing to tell her, actually. It was all vague.

The tired lips moved. "I will see my son alive," she said. "He starts down the cliff. There's that weapon in his hand; he goes down to kill that man—" Hate and loathing filled her voice. "That *explorer*." Smiling, she shut her eyes, and, imperceptably, passed back into sleep. The energy, the authority, had ebbed away. It could not be sustained, now.

After a moment Parsons tiptoed away, and out of the room.

Outside, Loris met him. "She's an incredibly strong person," he murmured, still under her spell.

"You told her?" Loris said.

"There was damn little to tell her," he said, feeling futile. "Except that I want to go back."

"Does she intend to try to come this time?"

"Yes," he said.

"Then we'll have to let her. Nobody would go against her decision. You know her; you've felt her power." Loris raised her hands in bitter resignation. "You can't blame her. We all want to see him, I, Jepthe, the old lady . . . we get a second to see him in all his glory, running down the cliff with that gun. And then—" She shuddered.

Parsons thought, But it's hard to feel sorry for a man who had murder in mind. After all, Corith was on his way down to kill.

On the other hand, Drake had certainly sent a good number of heavily armored Spanish soldiers over the side to drown; weighed down, those men had had no chance. Drake, to them, was simply a pirate. And in a sense they were right.

"We've made good progress in getting ready," Loris said, as they walked together along the corridor. "We've had more experience, now." Her voice was heavy with despair. "Do you want to see?"

This time, he was permitted to descend to the subsurface levels. At last he had been let in on all that the Wolf Clan had; nothing was kept back.

"You'll have to go further than the rest of us," Loris said, as they stepped from the lift. "In the way of altering your appearance. Because of your white skin. Our problem is one of costume. And keeping our equipment out of sight."

Ahead of him stood a group of men and women wearing furs and moccasins. It was difficult to accept the fact that such primitive-looking people were spurious. With a shock he identified Helmar among the group. All of them, their faces somber, hair braided back, had an ominous, warlike cast, an air of anger and distrust about them. An illusion, he decided, produced by their costumes.

The burnished red of their skins glowed in the artificial light that reflected throughout this subsurface chamber. That was natural, the fine, impressive red. He glanced at his own arms. How different he felt from them . . . what a contrast.

"You'll be all right," Loris said. "We have pigments."

"I have my own," he said. "In my instrument case."

By himself, in a side room, he removed all his clothing. This time he rubbed the pigment onto every part of him; he did not leave the telltale middle area white, as he had before. Then, with the help of several servants, he dyed his hair black.

"That isn't enough," Loris said, entering the room.

Startled, he said, "I haven't got anything on. He stood naked, the reddish pigment drying on him, with the servants braiding artificial hair into his, to give length to it. Loris, however, did not seem to care. She paid scarcely any attention to him.

"You must remember your eyes," she said. "They are blue."

With contact lenses, the pupils of his eyes were given a dark brown cast.

"Now look at yourself in the mirror," Loris said. A full-length mirror was produced, and Parsons studied himself in it. Meanwhile, the servants began to dress him in the furs. Loris watched critically, seeing to it that each part of his garments was placed on him properly.

"How about it?" he said. The man in the mirror moved when he moved; he had trouble accepting the image as his, this frowning, bare-armed, bare-legged warrior, with his coppery skin, his greasy-looking uncut hair falling down the back of his neck.

"Fine," Loris said. "It isn't important that we be authentic, but that we fit the sixteenth century English stereotype of Indians—they're the ones we have to deceive. They kept several armed scouts posted here and there on the cliffs overlooking their careened ship."

"What's the relationship between Drake's party and the local Indians?" Parsons asked.

"Evidently good. He has been plundering Spanish ships to his heart's content, so there is plenty of valuable material aboard—no need of ravaging the countryside. To him and his men, the California Coast area has no value; he's there because after he successfully plundered the Spanish ships near Chile and Peru, he went north seeking a passage to the Atlantic."

"So in other words," Parsons said, "he's not there for conquest. At least, not against the Indians. It's been other whites that he's preyed on."

"Yes," she admitted. "And now that you are all ready, I think we had better be getting back to the others."

As they walked back to join the group, Loris asked, "In case of emergency, you're familiar enough with the controls of our time ship so that you could operate it?"

"I hope so," he said.

Loris said, "You can be killed there, in Nova Albion."

"Yes," he said, thinking of the lifeless figure floating and drifting silently, unchangingly in the cold-pack. And, he thought, if anything went wrong, if we're not able to get back to our own centuries . . .

We would be catching abalone and mussels. Living on elk and deer and quail.

These people could extol the virtues of Indian culture, but certainly they themselves would be unable to endure it. With an eerie awareness he thought, They would probably try to get back to England with Drake's men.

And, he thought, *so would I.*

The "Plate of Brasse" which Drake's men had left on the California Coast had been found forty miles north of San Francisco Bay. The *Golden Hind* had cruised up and down a considerable part of the coast before Drake, an expert and provident seaman, had found a harbor that suited him. The ship needed its rotten planks repaired, its bottom breamed, for the voyage across the Pacific back to England; it was loaded with enormous treasure, enough to transform the economy of the home country. To insure safety for the men and ship during the careenage, Drake needed a harbor that would give him as much privacy and freedom as possible. At last he found that harbor, with white cliffs, fog, much like the Sussex Coast that he knew so well. The ship was brought into the Estero, its cargo removed, and the careening begun.

Standing on the cliff, several miles from the Estero, Jim Parsons watched the work through high-powered prismatic binoculars.

Ropes from the ship trailed out into the water where they were attached to stakes driven deep and out of sight. The ship, on its side, lay like some injured animal washed up onto the beach, helpless and unable to get back to its element. Out in the water, several winches controlled the angle of the ship. The seaman at work replacing rotten planks stood on a wooden platform that kept them, at high tide, above the water level. Through his binoculars, Parsons saw them working with what appeared to be pots of tar or pitch; fires smoldering beneath the pots, and the men carried the tar to the side of the ship by means of broomlike poles. The men wore cloth trousers, rolled up, and cloth shirts, washed a light blue. Their hair, in the warm, midday sun, shone yellow.

To his ears came the distant, faint noises of their voices.

He saw no sign of Drake himself.

Surveying the Estro, Parsons tried to recall what had become of this region in his own time. A subdivision of tract houses called Oko Village, named after the twentieth century realtor who had financed it. And a resort frontage along the water's edge: private beaches and boats.

"Where is Drake?" he said, crouching down beside Helmar and Loris and the others in their fur wrappers.

"Off somewhere in a dinghy," Helmar said. "Scouting."

Behind them, the time ship had been hidden among trees, covered with shrubbery and branches to disguise its metal exterior. Now, as Parsons glanced back at it, he saw that they were bringing out the old woman in her chair. With her was her daughter, Jepthe, the wife of her son. The old woman, wrapped in a black wool shawl, complained in a shrill peevish voice as the chair bumped over the uneven ground.

"Can't she be kept more quiet?" he said softly to Loris.

"This excites her," Loris said. "They won't hear. Sound travels up here because it's reflected by the water and cliffs. She knows that she has to be careful."

The old woman, as her chair neared the cliff edge, became silent.

"What are we supposed to do?" Loris said to Parsons.

He said, "I don't know." He did not know what he himself was supposed to do. If he could sight

Drake . . . "You're sure he's not aboard the ship," he said.

With a sardonic twitch of his lips, Helmar said, "Look along the cliff."

Turning his glasses, Parsons saw, hidden among the rocks, a small group of figures. Red arms, shiny black hair, the gray fur of their garments. Both men and women.

"Ourselves," Helmar said hoarsely. "The previous time."

In the binoculars, Parsons saw a woman rise up slightly, a powerfully built woman whose strong neck glistened in the heat. Her head turned and he recognized Loris.

And, further along, also perched in a declivity of rock, another group. Through the glasses he once more identified Loris, and, with her, Helmar and the others. Beyond that, he could not see.

He said to Loris beside him, "Where is your father?"

"He left Nixina and Jepthe at the time ship," she said tonelessly. "He made them wait there while he started along the cliff. For quite a time they lost sight of him. When he reappeared he had changed to his costume and he was about one-third of the way down the face of the cliff. He disappeared behind some rocks, and then—" Her voice broke. Presently she resumed. "Anyhow, they saw him jump up, just for a second, and go over head-first with a yell. Whether the arrow had gotten him at that point we don't know. They next saw him roll down until he came to rest against a shrub growing from the face of the cliff. They hurried to the edge and managed to get down to him. And of course when they got to him they found him with the arrow in his heart."

Now she ceased talking. Helmar finished, "They saw no one else. But of course they were too busy trying to get the ship close enough to get him into it. They managed to land the ship on the cliff face, using its jets to support it until they had him inside."

"Was he dead?" Parsons asked.

"Dying," Helmar said matter-of-factly. "He lived for several minutes. But he wasn't conscious."

Loris touched Parsons' arm. "Look down again," she said.

Again he studied the Estro far below.

A small boat with five men in it had appeared from the far side of the careened ship. Methodically, it moved along, with four of the men working long oars. The fifth man, bearded, had some kind of metal instrument in his hand; Parsons saw it glint in the sun.

The man was Drake.

Yes, Parsons thought. But was it Stenog? He saw only the head, the beard, the man's clothes; the face was obscured, and too far away. If that is Stenog, he said to himself, then this is a trap, a fake. They are waiting. And they have weapons as good as ours.

"What weapons do they have?" he asked.

Loris said, "We understand that they have cutlasses, of course. And wheel-lock rifles, or possibly the older matchlock rifles. It is possible that some rifles have spiral grooves in the barrels, but that's only conjecture. They can't possibly fire this far in any case. There are a few cannon, removed from the ship—or at least we assume there are. We have seen none on the beach, however, and if they're still aboard the ship they certainly can't be fired. Not with the ship on its side. They took everything possible off to lighten the ship, so it would draw the least water. In any case, they have never fired on us, either with hand weapons or cannon."

They didn't have to, Parsons thought. At least, not with the weapons that Loris supposed. He said aloud, "So Corith went down the cliff assuming he was not in jeopardy."

"Yes," she said. "But Drake's men wouldn't be using an Indian weapon, would they?" The doubt, the bewilderment, showed in both her voice and face. This catastrophe made no sense to her; now, as before, it was beyond them. With the information they had, they could not deal with it. "Any why would a native kill him?" Loris demanded.

Below them, the small boat had begun pushing away from the *Golden Hind*. It moved gradually to the south, in their direction. Presently it would pass directly beneath their spot.

Parsons said, "I'm going down." Handing her the binoculars, he took the coil of rope that they had brought and began lashing one end to a well-secured rock. Helmar helped him, and together they got the rope tight. Then, taking the coil, Parsons started away from the group.

Almost at once he realized that he could not descend directly. Even if the rope were long enough to let him down to the beach, he would be conspicuous, dangling against the white cliff; the men in the boat would be aware of him. Leaving the rope, he scrambled back up to the top of the cliff and began to run. Ahead of him he made out a deep cleft, overgrown with shrubbery, a tangle of broken rocks and roots that dipped out of sight beneath him.

Catching hold, he crept down, step by step. Below, the Pacific seemed perfectly flat, spread out as far as the eye could see; the ocean and the cliffs—nothing else. The blue of the water, the crumbling rock in his hands as he clawed his way down. Now, for an instant, he caught sight of the small boat once more. The men rowing. Ribbon of sand, with foam and breakers, driftwood washed up. The disorderly collections of seaweed . . .

He stumbled and almost fell. Head-first, he hung, clutching at roots. Rocks and bits of shrubbery rained past him, falling somewhere. He could hear the sound echo.

Far below, the boat continued on. Silently. None of the tiny figures seemed to hear or notice.

Parsons, by degrees, righted himself. Facing the cliff, not looking at the ocean below, he again descended.

When next he halted, getting his wind, he saw that the boat had come closer to shore. Two of the men had gotten out and were wading in the surf.

Had they seen him?

Swiftly, he made his way down. The rock surface

became smooth; he clung for an interval, and then, taking a deep, prayerful breath, he released his grip and dropped. Beneath him, the sand rose. He struck and fell, his legs thrashing with pain. Rolling, he slid down among the seaweed and lay, wheezing, enduring the gradually declining numbness of impact.

The boat had been dragged up onto the shore. The men were searching for something on the beach, kicking at the sand. Some lost tool or instrument, Parsons thought. He lay stretched out, watching.

One of the men came toward him. And, after him, Drake. Both men passed directly in front of Parsons, and, as Drake turned, Parsons saw his face clearly, outlined against the sky.

Scrambling up, Parsons said, "Stenog!"

The bearded man turned. His mouth fell open with astonishment. The other men froze.

"You *are* Stenog," Parsons said. It was true. The man stared at him without recognition. "Don't you remember me? Parsons said grimly. "The doctor who cured the girl, Icara."

Now recognition came. The expression on the bearded man's face changed.

Stenog smiled.

Why? Parsons wondered. Why is he smiling?

"They got you out of the prison rocket, did they," Stenog said. "We thought so. One dead *shupo* and two unidentified corpses out of nowhere, sealed in and traveling back and forth." His smile grew, a knowing, confident smile. "I'm surprised to see you—you completely threw me off. How interesting . . . you here." His white, even teeth showed; he had begun to laugh.

"Why are you laughing?" Parsons demanded.

"Let's see your friend," Stenog said. "The one who's going to do the killing. Send him down." He put his hands on his hips, his legs wide apart. "I'm waiting."

FOURTEEN

LIKE a voice in a nightmare, the laughter followed after Parsons as he raced along the base of the cliff.

I was right, he thought.

Pausing once, he looked back. There on the beach, Stenog and his men waited for Corith. From the sand they had fished up what they had been searching for, a deadly, gleaming little weapon.

They had managed to complete the time-travel experiments.

Catching hold of roots and branches, Parsons scrambled up the cliff wall. I have to get to him first, he thought. I have to warn him. Rocks tumbled away; he sprawled and rolled back, clutching.

The figures below became smaller. They made no move to follow him.

Why don't they shoot me? he asked himself.

Now a ledge of rock came between him and Stenog. Gasping, he rested for a minute, out of sight, protected. But he had to go on. Struggling up, he seized a tree root and continued on up.

Don't they think I can stop him? he wondered. Is it fore-ordained that he will go through his cycle, be killed no matter what I do?

Am I going to fail?

Now, reaching out, he managed to catch hold of the turf at the crest of the cliff. He was able to pitch himself up onto the level ground. But at once he was up again, on his feet.

Where was Corith?

Somewhere. Not far off.

Trees grew ahead, a grove of wind-bent pines. He entered the grove, panting for breath. Back and forth he ran, searching among the trees.

I can't blame Stenog, he thought. He's protecting his society. It's his job.

And this is my job, he realized. To save my patient. The man I was called on to heal.

He stopped now, winded, unable to go on. Sinking down, he sat in the damp grass, in the shadows, resting and recovering. His fur garments were torn from scrambling up the cliff. Drops of blood oozed from his arm; he wiped it off on the grass.

Strange, he thought. Stenog, with his dark skin dyed white, masquerading as a white man. And myself, with my white skin dyed dark, masquerading as an Indian.

And—a white man struggling to help Corith kill Drake. And Stenog on the other side, taking Drake's place.

Or not taking Drake's place. But actually Drake. Is there an authentic Drake? Or is Stenog Drake? Was there another man, actually born in England in the early sixteenth century, named Francis Drake? Or has Stenog always been Drake? And there is no other person.

If there is another Drake, a real Drake, then where is he?

One thing he knew: the engraving and portrait had been made of Al Stenog, with beard and white skin, in Drake's place. So Stenog, not Drake, had come back to England from the New World with the plunder, and been knighted by the Queen. But had Stenog then continued to be Drake for the rest of his life?

Had that been Stenog who fought the Spanish warships, later on, in the war against Spain?

Who had been the great navigator? Drake or Stenog?

An intuition . . . the exploits of those explorers. The

fantastic navigation and courage. Each of them: Cortez, Pizarro, Cabrillo . . . each of them a man transplanted from the future, an imposter. Using equipment from the future.

No wonder a handful of men had conquered Peru. And another handful, Mexico.

But he did not know. If Corith died while trying to reach Drake, there would be no reason for Stenog, for the government of the future, to go on. The man could die only once.

Parsons got shakily to his feet. He began to walk, preserving his strength. The man is here somewhere, he told himself. If I keep looking, I'll eventually find him. There's no need for a panic reaction; it's only a question of time.

Ahead of him, among the trees, someone moved.

Cautiously, he approached. He saw several figures . . . reddish skin, furs. Had he found him? Reaching out, he spread apart the foliage.

On the far side of a rise the metallic sphere of a time ship caught the afternoon sun.

One of them, he realized. But which one?

Not the one he himself had come in; that was hidden elsewhere, disguised with mud and branches. This one sat out in the open.

There would be at least four time ships.

Assuming that this trip was the last.

I wonder if I will ever make any more, he thought. If, like Loris and Nixina, I will come again and again. Like a ghost. Haunting this spot, seeking a way to change the flow of past events.

One of the figures turned, and Parsons saw—who? A woman he did not recognize. A handsome woman, in her thirties . . . like Loris, but not Loris. The woman's black hair tumbled down her bare shoulders, her strong chin raised as she stood listening. She wore a skirt of hide around her waist, an animal pelt. Her naked breasts glistened, swayed as she turned her body. A wild-eyed, fierce woman who now dropped, crouching, alert.

A second woman appeared. Elderly and frail. Hesitantly stepping from the time ship. Wrapped in heavy robes.

The younger woman was Jepthe. Loris' mother. At an earlier time. When she was here before.

Nixina said, in a voice familiar to Parsons, "Why did you let him get out of sight?"

"You know how he is," Jepthe shot back in a husky voice. "How could I stop him?" She leaped up, tossing her mane of hair back. "Maybe we should go to the cliff. We might find him again there."

I am back thirty-five years, Parsons realized. Loris has not been born.

Barefoot, Jepthe hurried from the ship, into the trees. Her long legs carried her quickly; she vanished almost at once, leaving the old woman to catch up.

"Wait for me!" Nixina called anxiously.

Reappearing, Jepthe said, "Hurry." She emerged from the trees to help her mother. "You shouldn't have come."

Watching the supple body, the energetic loins, Parsons thought, But she has already conceived. Loris is in her womb now, as I'm looking at her. And one day she will nurse at those superb breasts.

He began to hurry through the trees, back in the direction of the cliff. Corith had left his time ship; at least he knew that. The man was on his way, approaching what he imagined to be Drake.

Ahead of him, he saw the Pacific. He emerged on the cliff once more. The sunlight momentarily blinded him and he halted, shielding his eyes.

Far off, also on the cliff edge, he saw a single figure. A man, standing on the edge.

The man wore a loincloth. On his head a horned buffalo skull jutted up, covering him almost to his eyes. Black hair hung down from beneath the buffalo skull.

Parsons ran toward him.

The man did not seem aware of him. He bent down, gazing over the edge of the cliff, at the ship below. His enormous copper-colored body was splashed with paint streaks of blue and black and orange and yellow across his chest, his thighs, his shoulders, even his face. Over his back a pelt-covered mass was tied to him by a thong that passed over his chest and strapped beneath his armpits. Weapons there, Parsons decided. And binoculars. The man whipped a pair of binoculars from the pack on his back, and, squatting down, studied the beach.

Of all of them, Parsons thought, Corith had by far the best disguise. It was worthy of his great preparation, his months of secret effort. The magnificent buffalo skull, with tatters of skin flapping in the ocean wind. The blazing bands of paint slashed across his body. A warrior in the prime of life.

Now, lifting his head, Corith noticed him. Their eyes met. Parsons was face to face with him—with the living man. for the first time.

And, he wondered, the last?

Seeing him, Corith stuck the binoculars back into his pack. He did not seem alarmed; there was no fear on his face. His eyes flashed. The man's mouth was set, the teeth showing, almost a grin. Suddenly he sprang to the edge of the cliff. In an instant he had gone over the side; he had vanished.

"Corith!" Parsons shouted. The wind whipped his voice back at him. His lungs labored as he reached the spot, dropped down, saw the loose rock sliding where Corith had gone. The fanatic, cunning assassin had gotten away. Without knowing—or caring—who Parsons was or why he wanted him. Or how he had known his name.

Corith did not intend to stop for anything. He could not take the chance.

Making his way down, Parsons thought, I've lost him. The man had already gotten past him. Down the cliff side.

Why did I think I could stop him? he asked himself. When they failed. His mother, his son, his wife, his daughter—the family itself, the Wolf Tribe.

Sliding, half-falling, he reached a projection and halted. He could see no sign of the man.

On the beach, the small boat was still drawn up in the

surf. The five men had collected by their weapon, concealing it. The bearded man wandered away, glanced up, continued to roam. Pretending that he doesn't know, Parsons thought. The decoy.

Taking hold of an outcropping, Parsons started cautiously on. He turned about, to face the cliff . . .

A few feet from him, Corith crouched. The relentless eyes bored at him; the face, inflamed with conviction, glowed. Corith held a tube in his hands. An elongated version of the weapon familiar to Parsons. With this, no doubt, he intended to kill Drake.

"You called me by name," Corith said.

Parsons said, "Don't go down there."

"How do you know my name?"

"I know your mother," he said. "Nixina. Your wife, Jepthe."

"I've never seen you before," Corith said. His eyes flickered; he studied Parsons, licking at his lower lip. Poised to spring, Parsons realized. Ready to leap away and on down the cliff. But, he thought, he will kill me first. With that tube.

"I want to warn you," Parsons said. He felt dizzy; for a moment black flecks passed in front of him, and the cliff wavered and began receding. The glare of the sun, the stark white sand, the ocean . . . he sat listening to the noise of the surf. Over it he could hear Corith's breathing. The rapid, constricted spasms.

"Who are you?" Corith said.

"You don't know me," he said.

"Why shouldn't I go down there?"

"It's a trap. They're waiting for you."

The massive face quivered. Corith raised the tube that he held. "It doesn't matter."

"They have the same weapons you have," Parsons said.

"No," Corith said. "Wheel-lock rifles."

"That's not Drake down there."

Now the black eyes flamed furiously; the face became distorted.

Parsons said, "The man down there is Al Stenog."

To that, Corith said nothing. He did not seem to react.

"The Director of the Fountain," Parsons said.

After a long time, Corith said, "The Director of the Fountain is a woman named Lu Farns."

At that, Parsons stared.

Corith said, "You're lying to me. I've never heard of anybody named Stenog.

They sat crouched against the rock surface of the cliff, facing each other silently.

"Your speech," Corith said. "You have an accent."

Parsons' mind raced. The whole thing had a ring of madness in it. Who was Lu Farns? Why had Corith never heard of Stenog? And then he understood.

Thirty-five years had passed since Corith's death. Stenog was a young man, no more than twenty. He had not become Director until long after Corith's death; in fact, he had not even been alive when Corith died. The woman, Lu Farns, was undoubtedly the Director of the Fountain during Corith's lifetime.

Relaxing a little, Parsons said, "I'm from the future." His hands were still shaking; he tried to quiet them. "Your daughter—"

"My *daughter*." Corith echoed, with a mocking grimace.

"If you go any further down," Parsons said, "you'll be shot through the chest. Killed. Your body will be taken back to your own time, to the Wolf Lodge, and put into cold-pack. For thirty-five years your mother and your wife, and finally your daughter, will try to undo your death; they'll give up eventually and call me in."

Corith said, "I don't have any daughter."

"But you will," he said. "You do now, in fact, but you don't know it. Your wife has conceived."

With no indication that he had heard him, Corith said, "I must go down there and kill that man."

"If you want to kill him," Parsons said, "I'll tell you how you can do it. Not by going down there."

"How?" Corith said.

"In your own time. *Before he solves the problem of time travel and comes back here.*" That was the only way; he had worked it out in his mind, examined the alternatives. "Here, he knows. There, if you go back, he doesn't. He didn't know about you when I was with him; all he had was a series of conjectures to go on. Shrewd guesses. But he was able to put them together; they resumed time-travel experimentation, and finally they were successful." Leaning urgently toward Corith, he went on, "Those weapons that you have won't help you here because—"

He broke off. From the pack strapped to Corith's body something stuck up—something that made cold, bleak fright rise inside him.

"Your costume," he managed to say. "You constructed it yourself. No one else saw it." He reached toward Corith. Toward the pack. From the pack he took—

A handful of arrows. With flint tips. And feathered with familiar colors.

"Fakes," Parsons said. "Which you made as part of your disguise. To come back here."

Corith said, "Look at your arm."

"What?" he said, dazed.

"You're a white man," Corith said. "The dye has rubbed off where you got scratched." Suddenly he seized hold of Parsons' arm and rubbed at his flesh. The dye, moistened, rubbed away, leaving a spot of grayish white. Letting go of his arm, he caught hold of the artificial hair braided into Parsons'; in an instant he had torn the artificial hair away. He sat holding it in his hand.

And then, without a word, he sprang at Parsons.

Now I see, Parsons thought. He tumbled back over the lip of the rock and down the cliff side. Snatching, scrabbling, he managed to catch hold; his body dragged agonizingly against the rock. And then, above him, Corith appeared. The massive body descending.

Parsons rolled away, trying to avoid him. *No*, he thought. *I don't want to.* The copper-colored hands closed around his throat, and he felt the man's knee dig into him . . .

Against him, Corith sagged. Blood gushed, staining the ground as it gurgled and became pools. Parsons, with a violent effort, managed to struggle out from beneath the man. He held, now, only one arrow. And he did not have to turn Corith over to see where the other was. As the man had dropped onto him, he had propped the arrow upright and it had gone into his heart.

I killed him, Parsons thought. By accident.

Above, on the edge of the cliff, Jepthe appeared. They'll know, he realized. In a moment. And when they find out—

Pressing against the cliff, he moved away from the dying man, crawling along the rock surface until he could no longer see either the woman or Corith. Then, step by step, he began ascending the cliff.

He reached the top. No one was in sight. They had gone down to Corith, but they would be back up immediately.

His mind empty, he ran from the cliff, toward the grove of trees. Presently he was out of sight among them. Safe, he thought. No one will know; now they won't know.

The mystery of his death. They will never find out.

I did not intend to, he thought, but that makes no real difference. No wonder Stenog laughed. He knew it was going to be I who killed Corith.

Stopping, he stood deep in frantic thought.

I can go back to Loris and Helmar, he decided. Tell them that I saw only what they saw: Corith on the cliff, going down, and then Corith die. No one else. Nobody came up the cliff from below. The only ones who came down were Jepthe and Nixina. I don't know any more than they do.

And Corith will never tell, because he is dead.

Hiding, he heard voices. He saw Nixina and Jepthe rushing through the trees, searching for their time ship, their faces blank with grief. Going to get the ship, put him into it, take him back and get him into cold-pack.

Corith is dead, but thirty-five years from now he will be brought back to life. I will do it. I will be there, in the Lodge, responsible for his rebirth.

He knew, now, why the second arrow had appeared in Corith's chest. Why he had not remained alive.

The first time, he had killed Corith by accident. But not the second time. That would be on purpose.

I must have come back, he realized, in one of the time ships. That night that I revived Corith, while he lay unconscious, recuperating. While I was with Loris, I was also downstairs with him.

But why with an arrow?

He looked down at his hand. He still clutched one arrow. Scrambling up the cliff, he had hung onto it. Why? he asked himself.

Because the arrows saved my life. If I hadn't had them, Corith would have killed me. I was defending myself.

There had been no choice.

And yet, he felt dread, the horror of responsibility. He had been trapped, drawn into it against his will. Corith had leaped on him, and he had done nothing but struggle to protect himself.

What else could I have done? he asked himself. Surely it isn't my fault. But if not, then whose fault is it?

Who really was responsible for the crime? And it was a crime. Any killing is a crime. I'm a doctor, he said to himself. My job is to save human life. Especially this man's life.

But at the cost of my own? Because, when I revive him at the Lodge, he will point me out. And I will be helpless. Because I will not know; this has not happened to me yet.

FIFTEEN

STANDING alone in the woods, Parsons thought, I am the man they are searching for. Thirty-five years.

The people at the Lodge would kill him at once, as soon as Corith indicted him. They would show no mercy—and why should they?

Had he, himself?

Perhaps he could break the sequence at some point. Catch myself before I come back here, he thought. Before I kill him the first time.

Above his head, a metallic object moved swiftly, leaving the woods and going to the cliff. The object dropped beyond the edge of the cliff; he heard its jets roaring as it stabilized itself near Corith. The old woman and her daughter had gone to collect the dying man.

In the vicinity, he realized, there were three other time ships; four, if Stenog's was included. This one had already gone into motion, but the others remained. Or did they?

I have to get to one of them, he thought. He began running aimlessly, in panic. But the ships from past time-segments—he could not approach them without disrupting history. That left only Stenog's ship, and the one that he had arrived here in. Could he go back and face Loris and the others? Knowing that he had killed Corith?

He had to.

Coming out on the cliff, he began running back the

way he had originally come. As far as they're concerned, he told himself, this trip has simply been a failure. As before, no one has been able to make out what happened. I've given them no help. My plan was a failure. There is no choice but to give up and return to the future.

While he ran he saw, over the cliff, the tiny figures on the beach below. Stenog's men, at the boat.

The men, with their oars, were tracing huge letters in the sand. Parsons paused. And saw that the letters spelled out his name. Stenog was trying to signal him. With great speed, as if by some prearranged system, the men got their message completed as he stood gazing down.

PARSONS. THEY SAW, KNOW.

Warning him. That this time the trip had not been a total failure. So he could not go back after all.

Turning, he sprinted across the open space, back into the woods. Once they see me, he realized, they'll kill me. Or—his heart sank. They don't even have to do that. All they have to do is go back to the future without me. Leave me here.

But then I can go down to Stenog's ship, he realized.

Go down—and find himself in the hands of the government once more, to be shipped out of the prison colonies. Was that what he wanted? Was that better than remaining here, a castaway? At least he would be free here; he could certainly contact an Indian tribe in the area, survive with them . . . and, later on, when a ship from Europe arrived, he could go back with them. He racked his brains. What was the next contact between this region, Nova Albion, and the Old World? Something like 1595. A captain named Cermeno had wrecked—*would* wreck—his vessel off the entrance to the Estro. That was—sixteen years.

Sixteen years here, living on clams and deer, squatting around a fire, huddled in a tent made of animal hide, scratching at the soil for roots. This was the superlative culture that Corith wanted to preserve, in place of Elizabethan England.

Better, Parsons thought, to turn myself over to Stenog. He started back in the direction of the cliff.

Ahead of him, a figure emerged, stepped into his path. For one terrible instant he thought it was Corith. The powerful shoulders, the grim, rigid features, the sharp, hawklike nose . . .

It was Helmar. Corith's son.

Halting, Parsons faced him. Now Loris and Jepthe appeared.

By the expression on their faces, he saw that Stenog had not lied to him.

"He was on his way down to them," Helmar said to Loris.

Loris, her face stark, said, "You betrayed us."

"No," Parsons said. But he knew that it was pointless to try to talk to them.

"When did the idea come to you?" Loris said. "Back at the Lodge? Did you get us to bring you here so you could do it? Or did the idea come to you when you saw him?"

Parsons said, "The idea never came to me."

"You intercepted him," Loris said. "You went down and talked to Drake—you conferred with him. We saw you. And then you came up the cliff and stopped Corith and murdered him. And then you were going back down to Drake, to go back with him. He warned you that we saw; he had his men write in the sand. So you knew you couldn't go back to us."

To that, Parsons said nothing. He faced them silently.

Pointing his weapon at Parsons, Helmar said, "We're going back to the time ship."

"Why?" Parsons said. Why not kill me here? he wondered.

"Nixina has made the decision," Loris said.

"What decision?"

Loris, in a choked, constricted voice, said, "She thinks you didn't mean to do it. She says—" She broke off. "If you had meant to do it, you would have brought some kind of weapon with you. She thinks you stopped Corith to argue with him, and that he wouldn't listen to you. And you fought each other, and in the fight Corith was stabbed."

Parsons said, "I warned him not to go down." They

were listening, at least for a moment. "I told him," he said, "that it's not Drake down there. It's Stenog, waiting for him."

After a pause, Loris said, "And of course my father had never heard of Stenog. He didn't know what you meant." Bitterly, her lips twisting, she said, "And he saw the white showing on your arm. He knew you were a white man, and he didn't trust you; he wouldn't listen to you, and it cost him his life."

"Yes," Parsons said.

All of them were silent now.

"He was too suspicious," Loris said at last. "Unwilling to trust anyone. Nixina was right. You didn't mean to. It wasn't your fault. Any more than it was his." She raised her dark, grief-stricken eyes. "It *was* his fault in a sense. For being the way he was."

"There's no use thinking about that now," Jepthe said curtly.

"No," Loris agreed. "Well, there's nothing to do but go back. We failed."

Helmar said, "At least we know how it happened." He eyed Parsons with scorn and loathing.

"We'll abide by Nixina's decision," Jepthe said to him in a sharp, commanding voice.

"Yes," Helmar said, still staring fixedly at Parsons.

"What is her decision?" Parsons demanded.

Loris said, "We'll—" She hesitated. "Even if it was an accident," she said woodenly, "we feel that you should make some sort of atonement for it. We're going to leave you here. But not at this point in time." Her voice grew fainter. "A little further along."

With comprehension, Parsons said, "You mean after Drake's ship has left."

Helmar said, "You can spend your time trying to find that out." With his weapon, he indicated that he wanted Parsons to come toward them.

Together, they walked back along the cliff, to the time ship. Sitting in front of the ship, in her special chair, Nixina waited for them unseeingly. Several of the Wolf Tribe stood around her.

When they reached her, Parsons stopped. "I'm sorry," he said.

The old woman's head moved slightly, but she said nothing.

"Your son wouldn't listen to me," Parsons said.

After a time, Nixina said, "You shouldn't have stopped him. You weren't worthy to stop him."

Parsons thought. The blame has to be on me. For them to admit that Corith was responsible, through his fanaticism and paranoia—that would be too much for them. Psychologically, they could not stand it. So, he thought, I'm the scapegoat. I must be punished, as proof of my guilt.

Wordlessly, he entered the ship.

Trees.

He stood looking around him, trying to catch some indication of change. Blue sky, the distant boom of the surf . . .

All the same. Except—

As fast as possible, he made his way to the cliff. Below, the beach. Sand, seaweed, the Pacific. Nothing else.

The careenage had ended. The *Golden Hind* had gone.

Or—had not yet come.

How could he tell? Marks in the sand? The remains of the wooden stakes to which the ropes had been tied? Some debris of some sort would remain.

But what did it matter?

Maybe, he thought, I can find some way of getting south, down into Mexico, Cortez . . . when he landed?

The best I can hope for is to reach a friendly Indian tribe. If I'm lucky I can either live with them or persuade them to help me get south. But I can't remember if there are Spanish settlements yet. And I don't know what year this is, so even if I remembered, it would not help me. They could have moved me back a century. Or even several centuries. Ocean, rocks, trees—those remain the same for a thousand years.

I may be standing here two hundred years before the first white man lands in the New World.

He thought, In fact *I* may be the first white man in the New World.

At least, he could go down to the beach and see. If there were any debris left from the *Golden Hind*, it would prove that they had not moved him back in time. And that would be something. A faint hope—the Spanish colonies to the south. And then a ship back to Europe.

Once again, he began the slow, dangerous descent to the beach.

For an hour he searched up and down the beach, seeing no sign of the ship or the men ever having been there. No marks, no refuse. What about the brass plate? he asked himself. Where had Drake actually left it? Lying in the sand? Buried in the face of the cliff? He searched for that, but by now he had covered so much of the beach that he no longer had a central point from which to work. Possibly he had wandered a mile or so from his original spot. The beach all looked alike, now; cliff and sand and seaweed . . .

Suddenly he stopped in his tracks. *If he was stranded here, how did he manage to get back to the Wolf Lodge to kill Corith a second time?* All this had no importance; obviously he did get back to the Lodge. If not, then he would be removed from this place anyhow, by the new time-sequence set up by his failure to reach the recuperating Corith. And the only way he could get back to the Wolf Lodge was by means of a time ship. Obviously, some one came back to get him—would come back.

But how soon? He could spend years here, decades, become an old man, and then, after all that, one of them could return in a time ship and pick him up. Near the end of his life.

For instance, he might, over a period of years, work his way south to a Spanish settlement, and then back to Spain, up to England, where he would manage to make contact with Stenog. Eventually, in that manner, he could regain access to the future . . . a worn-out, fever-ravaged old man whose life was over. A man who had wandered the face of the globe, who had used up his life.

And of course it was always possible that someone else killed Corith the second time.

He noticed, now, that the day was ending. The air had become cold and the sun had moved to the edge of the sky. A few gulls flapped by overhead; their mournful cry, like the rubbing of ropes, made the scene even more lonely.

Night would come on soon. What would he do? He couldn't spend the night on the beach. Better to trudge back up and start inland, back across the peninsula; as he recalled, there had been Indian settlements on the inner bay, Tomales Bay, where it was more sheltered.

Standing on the beach, looking up at the cliff, he did not see a way to ascend; he would have to go along the beach, searching for one of the declivities, or a spot where trees and shrubs had grown. But he was too tired. I'll have to wait until tomorrow, he decided. He seated himself on a log that had been washed up on the beach, unlaced his moccasins, and rested his head on his arms. Closing his eyes, he listened to the surf and the croaking gulls. The inhuman, inhospitable sound . . . how many millions of years, more or less, had this sound gone on? Long before there had been any men. And long after.

He thought, It would be so easy to walk out into the water and not come back. Simply start walking.

The chill wind blew about him; he shivered. How long could he sit here? Not much longer. Opening his eyes he saw that it had become appreciably darker; the sun had now disappeared. Far off, a flight of birds disappeared beyond the hills to the north.

Like children, he thought. Punishing me by exiling me here. Unable to bear the blame themselves. And yet, in a sense, they were right. I should bear the blame; I was the agent responsible for his death. And if I had a chance to kill him again, I would. I wish to God I had that chance, he thought. He got up from the log and began walking along aimlessly, kicking at shells on the sand ahead of him.

A large rock crashed noisily down the cliff side; involuntarily, he jumped away. The rock rolled out onto the beach, along with a shower of smaller stones. Shading his eyes, he peered up.

A figure stood at the top of the cliff, waving to him. The figure cupped its hands to its mouth and called something, but the boom of the surf blotted it out. He saw only the outline of the figure; he could not tell if it was a man or a woman or what it wore. At once he began frantically waving back.

"Help!" he shouted. He ran toward the cliff, indicating that he could not climb up. Now he scampered along, half-falling, trying to find a way up.

Above him, the figure made motions that he could not grasp. He halted, panting for breath, trying to make out what it was telling him. Then the figure abruptly disappeared. One moment it was there; the next it was gone. He blinked in bewilderment, feeling slow terror creep over him. The person had turned away from the cliff and gone off.

Frozen with disbelief, he remained where he was, unable to stir. And, while he stood there, a metallic sphere rose from the top of the cliff and rapidly floated down to the beach.

The time ship landed on the sand ahead of him. Who would come out? He waited, his heart laboring.

The door opened and Loris appeared. She did not wear the Indian costume now; she had changed back to the gray robe of the Wolves. Her face had lost most of its shock and grief; he realized that for her considerable time had passed.

"Hello, Doctor," she said.

He could only gaze mutely at her.

"I came back for you," she said. She added, "It's a month or so later. I'm sorry it took so long. How long has it been for you? You haven't got any beard, and your clothes look about the same . . . I hope it's the same day."

"Yes," he said, hearing his voice grate out harshly.

"Come on," she said, beckoning him toward her. "Get in. I'll take you back, Doctor. To your own time. To your wife." She smiled at him, a forced smile. "You don't deserve to be left here." She added, "Nobody from your civilization would ever find you here. Helmar saw to that. This is 1597. No one will come here for a long, long time."

Trembling, he stepped into the time ship.

After she had closed the door behind him, he said, "What made you change your mind?"

Loris said, "You'll find out some day. It has to do with something that you and I did together. Something that didn't seem important at the time." Again she smiled at him, but this time it was an enigmatic, almost caressing smile on her full, dark lips.

"I appreciate it," he said.

"Do you want me to take you directly back?" she asked, as she began to operate the controls. "Or is there anything from our period that you need? I have your instrument case here." She pointed, and he saw, on the floor of the time ship, his familiar gray case.

With difficulty, he said, "I'd like to go back to the Lodge for a little while. To get cleaned up. Change my clothes, rest. I don't want to return to my family this way." He indicated the ragged fur costume, the remains of the dye. "They'll think it's a wild man escaped from the zoo."

"Of course," Loris said, in the formal, civil way that he had become familiar with. The aristocratic politeness. "We'll go back to my time; you'll be given whatever you need. Of course, you'll have to stay out of sight. No one else must see you. But you understand that. I'll take you directly to my apartment."

"Fine," he said. And he thought with a rush of misery, It's her father that I'm going back for. To complete what I have to do. How will she feel is she ever finds out? Maybe she never will. If I can get use of the time machine for even a second . . .

She saved me, he thought, so that I can murder her father. For the second time.

Silently, he sat watching her manipulate the controls.

SIXTEEN

THE TIME SHIP came to rest in an enclosed courtyard paved with cobblestones. Parsons, as he stepped from the ship, saw the iron railings of vaulted balconies, damp foliage of plants, and then Loris led him through a doorway and along a deserted corridor.

"This part of the Lodge," she said over her shoulder to him, "is mine. So you don't need to worry; no one will interfere with us."

Soon he lay in a bathtub of hot water, his head against the porcelain side, eyes shut, enjoying the smell of soap and the peace and silence of the room.

Almost at once the door opened and Loris entered with an armload of washcloths and towels. "Sorry to bother you," she said, folding a fluffy white bathtowel over a rack on the wall.

He did not answer. He did not even open his eyes.

"You're tired," she said. Lingering, she said, "I know now why none of our signal markers reached you."

At that, he opened his eyes.

"That first trip you took," she said. "To the far future. When you didn't know how to operate the ship."

"What happened to the markers?"

She said, "Helmar destroyed them."

"Why?" he said, wide awake.

Brushing her long black hair from her eyes she said calmly, "We sought any possible way to break the chain

134

at some point. You understand—very few of us have any well-disposed feelings toward you." She hesitated, considering him as he lay in the tub. "Odd," she said, "to have you back here. You're going to spend the night with me, aren't you?"

He said, "So Helmar did what he could to leave me trapped in the future." He thought. It was not bad enough for me, back in the past, in Nova Albion. Recalling the desolate plains of the future, his body and mind recoiled. And they had done their best. If it had not been for the plaque . . . Abruptly he said, "And he tried to find the granite plaque, too?"

"He searched," Loris said. "But he failed to find it. There was some doubt in our minds—quite a bit in Helmar's—that there ever was any plaque. All the signal markers were located; there was no real trouble in doing that, since we knew exactly where they were, and how many we had sent out. Helmar returned, but it made no difference. My father—" She shrugged, her arms folded. "It had no effect on him."

After his bath, he dried himself. He shaved, and then, putting on a silk robe that Loris had presented to him, came out of the bathroom.

On a chair in the corner of the bedroom, Loris sat curled up, her feet bare; she wore Chinese coolie trousers and a white cotton shirt. On her wrists were heavy silver bracelets. And she had tied her hair back in a pony tail. She seemed pensive and taciturn.

"What is it?" he said.

She glanced up. "I'll be sorry to see you go. I wish—" All at once she slid from the chair and paced about the room, her fingers stuck in the side pockets of her light blue trousers. "I want to tell you something, Doctor. But I shouldn't. Maybe some day." Turning swiftly, she said, "I think a great deal of you. You're a fine person."

He thought, She is making it hard for me. Excruciatingly hard. I wonder if I can do it. But there is no alternative that I know of.

His clothes had been carefully put up on a shelf of the closet. Now he got them down.

"What are you going to do?" Loris said, watching him. "Aren't you going to bed?" She showed him the pajamas that she had for him.

"No," he said, "I want to be up awhile."

After he had dressed he stood indecisively at the door of the apartment.

"You're so tense," Loris said. "Does it frighten you to be here, in the Lodge? You're not afraid Helmar will come bursting in, are you?" Going past him—he smelled the warm fragrance of her hair—she bolted the door to the outer hall. "Nobody can come in here; this is sacred. The queen's bedroom." She smiled, showing her regular, white teeth. "Enjoy yourself," she said gently, putting her hand on his arm. "This will be your last time, my dear." Leaning forward, she kissed him on the mouth with great tenderness.

"I'm sorry," he said. And unbolted the door.

"Where are you going?" Now her face filled with wariness. "You're going to do something. What is it?" At once she slipped by him, catlike, barring his passage. Her eyes glowing, she said, "I won't let you go. You want to get revenge on Helmar, do you? Is that it?" She studied him, "No, that's not it. But what can it be?"

Putting his hands on her shoulders, he moved her aside. Her powerful, healthy body resisted; for a moment she tugged at his hands, and then suddenly, on her face, comprehension appeared.

"Oh God," she whispered. The color left her face; the burnished red faded, and he saw, for an instant, the haggard, desolate face of an old woman. "Doctor," she said. "Please don't."

He started to open the door.

At once she was on him. Her fingers raked at his face, tearing at his flesh, clawing at his eyes. His arms came up instinctively and he flung her backward; she clung to him, pulling him down, dragging at him with the strength and weight of her body. Her white teeth flashed; she bit him frenziedly on the neck. With his other arm he struck her across the face and she dropped away, gasping hoarsely.

Rapidly, he stepped out of the apartment, into the hall.

"Stop," she snarled, coming after him. From her shirt she tugged something, a slender metal tube; he saw it, and then he lashed out. His fist caught her on the side of the jaw, but she avoided the force of the blow; her eyes glazed with pain, but she did not fall. The tube wavered, and he grabbed at it. Instantly she yanked back, away from him; he saw the tube pointed at him, and the look on her face. The suffering. Raising her hand, drawing it back, she flung the tube at him, sobbing.

The tube fell to the floor near his feet and rolled away.

"Goddamn you," she moaned, covering her face with her hands. She turned away, her back to him; he saw the convulsions that racked her. "Go on," she cried, again turning toward him, tears spilling down her cheeks.

Swiftly, he ran down the hall, the way they had come. He came out onto the darkened courtyard. There, dimly, he saw the outline of the metal ship. As quickly as possible he entered it, slammed and locked the door.

Could he operate it? Seating himself, he inspected the dials. Then, summoning his memory, he clicked on a toggle switch.

The machinery hummed. Dials swung to register.

He closed a switch and then, hesitating, pressed a button.

A dial showed that he had gone back half an hour in time. That gave him half an hour to make a thorough study of the dials, to recover his earlier knowledge.

Calming himself, he began his scrutiny.

At a period of one day and a half in the past, he stopped the mechanism. With caution, he unlocked the door of the ship and swung it open.

No one was in sight.

Stepping out, he made his way across the courtyard. He swung up onto a balcony and stood, pondering.

First, he had to get one of Corith's arrows.

Down beneath the ground, in the first subsurface level, he would find the workroom in which Corith had constructed his costume. But did the arrows still exist there? A few were far back in the past, at Nova Albion. One, which he had pulled from Corith's chest, was here somewhere in the Lodge, unless it had been destroyed.

Did Corith die the second time from the *same* arrow?

Now he remembered. That arrow had been disassembled; he had removed the flint head, the feathers, to analyze them. So his second death could not have come from that arrow; it had to be one of the others. And that second arrow was not, like the first, removed. At least, not to his knowledge.

The time was evidently quite late at night. Almost morning. The halls, artificially lighted, seemed deserted.

With infinite caution, he made his way down to the first subsurface level.

For an hour he searched in vain for one of Corith's arrows. At last he gave up. Now the clocks on the walls of the various chambers read five-thirty; the Lodge would soon be awake.

He had no choice but to go back into the past for the arrow.

Returning to the time ship, he locked himself inside and again seated himself at the controls.

This time he sent himself and the ship back thirty-five years. Before Loris' birth. Before either she or Helmar existed. And, he hoped, before Corith left for his ill-fated encounter in the far past.

Again, he had arrived late at night. He had no difficulty locating the Lodge's subsurface work area of that period, its machine shops. But Corith's workroom was, of course, securely locked. It took skillful use of the time ship before he located a moment at which he could enter. But he at last found such a moment. The door of the workroom hung open, and no one was inside. In need of a particular tool, Corith had gone off; he caught a glimpse of the man leaving, and an inspection of the near future showed that he would not return for at least two hours.

Entering, he found half-finished costumes here and there, and, on a work bench, the buffalo head. Pigments, photographs of the Indian tribes of the past—he roamed about, examining everything. There, by a lathe, he found three arrowss. Only one had its flint head in place. With an odd feeling he picked up a chisel that Corith had been using. And here was the raw flint, too. He noticed the textbook on Stone Age artifacts that Corith had employed as his guide; the heavy book was propped up against the wall, held open with a block of wood.

The book—written in English—had been pilfered from the library of the University of California. It was due back on March 12, 1938, and after that the borrower would be fined.

Instead of the one finished arrow, he selected one in process, reasoning that Corith would not as readily notice its absence. By scrutinizing the book and the finished arrows, he was able to see how the flint and the feathers were secured in place.

Seating himself at the bench, he finished making the arrow. It took him well over an hour. I wonder if I've done as good a job as Corith, he asked himself.

Taking his completed arrow, he cautiously left the workroom and made his way from the subsurface level, up the ramp and along the corridors, to the time ship. Again, no one saw him; he reached the ship safely and re-entered.

And now, he thought, there is nothing more. Only the act itself. Can I do it? I have to, he realized.

I already have done it.

With precision, he selected the exact time, the period to which Corith lay recuperating from the operation which Parsons himself had performed. Again and again, he checked the settings on his dials. If he made an error at this point . . .

But he knew, with leaden hopelessness, that he would not—had not—made an error.

Wrapping the arrow, he placed it inside his shirt.

This trip he had to move in space as well as time. The room in which Corith lay was well guarded; he could not get in without being noticed and recognized. Of course, the guards would admit him, but later they would remember. He had to emerge within the room itself, close by the patient's bed.

Now, with equal precision, he began setting the controls that would relocate the ship in space. A nexus of the two, time and space, a point on the graph . . .

The control board hummed. Dials registered. And then the self-regulating banks of equipment clicked off. The trip had ended; according to the indicators, he had arrived.

At once he flung open the door of the time ship.

A room, familiar, with white walls. To his left, a bed on which lay a man, a dark-faced man with powerful features, eyes shut.

He had succeeded!

Going to the bed, Parsons bent down. He had only seconds; he could not pause. Now he brought out the arrow and stripped the wrappings from it.

On the bed, the man breathed shallowly. His large, strong hands lay at his sides, copper against the white of the sheets. His thick black hair spilled down over the pillow.

Again, Parsons thought. As if once was not enough, for both of us. Shaking, he raised the arrow back, gripping its shaft with both hands. Can I penetrate the ribs this way? he asked himself. Yes. The soft, vulnerable area around the heart . . . he had laid it open in order to perform the operation.

Good God, he realized with horror. He had to drive the arrow into that spot, into the newly-stitched tissue that he had only a short while ago repaired. The sardonic irony . . .

Below him, Corith's eyes fluttered. His breathing changed. And, as Parsons stood holding the arrow, Corith opened his eyes.

He gazed up at Parsons. The eyes, empty, saw nothing at first. And then, imperceptibly, consciousness came. The slack lines of the man's tired face altered, gained force.

Parsons started to bring the arrow down. But his hand wobbled; he had to draw the arrow back once again, to start over.

Now the dark eyes fixed themselves on him. The man's mouth opened; the lips drew back as Corith tried to speak.

After thirty-five years, Parsons thought. To come back to life, for this.

Corith lifted his hand from the sheet, raising it an inch and then letting it fall back. "You, once more . . ." Corith whispered.

"I'm sorry," Parsons said.

There was comprehension in the dark eyes. He seemed aware of the arrow. Again he put up his hand, as if reaching for it. But he did not take his eyes from Parsons. Faintly, he said, "You've been against me . . . from the start." The frail chest heaved beneath the sheet. "Spying on me as I worked . . . lying to me . . . pretending to be on my side." Now the weak, trembling hands touched the arrow, and then fell away. Consciousness ebbed; he gazed at Parsons wonderingly, with the vacant, troubled gaze of a child.

I can't do it, Parsons realized.

My entire life, everything that I've ever been and stand for, prohibits me. Even if it means my own death; even though, when this man awakens, he will name me, point me out, get his fanatic, paranoid revenge. Parsons lowered the arrow, and then dropped it to the floor, away from the bed.

He felt utter, numbing fear. And defeat.

So now this man can go on, he thought. Standing by the bed, looking down at Corith, he thought, There is nothing to stop him. A madman. He will destroy me first, and then go on to the rest of his "enemies." But I still can't do it.

Turning from the bed, he walked unsteadily back to the time ship, entered, and bolted the door after him. But there's no safety in here, he realized. Snapping on the bank of controls, he moved the ship ahead in time two hours. Two hours or two thousand years; it made no difference. Not with Corith alive. Not for that other, earlier Parsons, sitting with Loris, waiting for his patient to regain consciousness.

Now the past can unravel. Now the new chain of cause and effect can begin. Starting from that moment, at the bed, when I failed to drive the arrow into the man's chest. When I let him live. A whole new world, built up from that moment on. Unwinding, carrying itself forward with its own dynamic force.

Shutting off the controls of the time ship, he stood hesitantly at the door. Shall I see? he asked himself. Corith regaining consciousness, his wife and son and daughter and mother around him . . . and myself there, too. All of us pleased. Gratified. Bending to hear his every word.

Can I watch?

Strange . . . that he was still here. He had expected the change to set in at once, as soon as he moved away from the bed.

Now he had to look—without delay.

Tearing open the door of the time ship, he peered out at a scene that he had lived through once before. People at the bedside, their backs to him, paying no attention to him. The elaborate machinery of the Lodge's soul cube, the pumps that activated the cold-pack. Already, they had gotten Corith back into the cold-pack; he saw their grief-stricken faces, and then the man himself, drifting in the familiar medium.

The arrow, as before, projected from his chest.

Instantly, Parsons slammed the door of the time ship; he punched dials and sent the ship randomly into time, away from the scene. Had they noticed him? Evidently not; the room had been chaotic with activity, men coming and leaving, and himself—he had seen himself standing by the soul cube with Loris, both of them lost in the shock of the moment. Neither of them able to understand or explain—or even accept—what had happened.

He felt that way now.

Shaken, he sat at the controls. So it was not I, he realized. I didn't kill him. Someone else did, the second time.

But who?

He had to go back. To see. After he had left the room, gone back into his time ship, someone else had arrived. Loris? But she had been with him during that period, they had been together when Helmar brought the news. Helmar?

If Corith returned to life, Helmar would be supplanted. For the first time in his life. His potent father, returning . . . and Corith would easily dominate the Wolf Tribe; Helmar would shrink to nothing. Or—

Step by step, he began methodically setting the controls of the time ship.

Who would he see when he opened the door? He steered himself against the sight. Calculating down to seconds, he brought the ship to a point in time immediately following the moment at which he had left. There would be no gaps; he would be present during the whole sequence. It must have happened almost at once, he decided. As soon as I left, someone else came in. Someone opened the door of the room and slipped inside. Possibly they saw me; he or she was waiting for me to leave.

Throwing the controls to *off,* he jumped to his feet, ran to the door of the ship and opened it, looked out into the room.

At the bed two figures stood. A man and a woman, bending over the prone figure of Corith. The man's arm flashed up; it came down, and the act had been accomplished. Swiftly, the man and the woman retreated from the bed, silently, already in flight. They wasted no time; their movements were expert and orderly. Obviously, every step had been well planned long in advance. Their tense, strained faces confronted him as they turned.

He had never seen either of them before. Both the man and the woman were total strangers to him.

They were young. No more than eighteen or nineteen, with firm, smooth faces, skin almost as light as his own. The woman's hair was wheat-colored, her eyes blue. The man, somewhat darker, had heavier brows and almost black hair. But both of them had the same finely made cheek bones and molded jaw-lines; he saw the resemblance between them. The spark, the alertness and clarity, in their gaze. The high order of intelligence.

The woman—or girl—reminded him of Loris. She had Loris' carriage, her well-made shoulders and hips. And the man also had familiar lines in his body.

"Hello," the girl said.

Both of them wore the gray robes of the Wolf Tribe. But not the emblem. On their breasts a new emblem stood out: crossed snakes twining up a staff topped by open wings. The caduceus. The ancient sign of the medical profession.

The boy said, "Doctor, we should get out of here at once. Will you let my sister go in your ship?" He pointed, and Parsons saw, beside his own ship, a second identical metallic sphere with its door hanging open. "We'll meet ahead in time; Grace knows the point." He smiled briefly at Parsons as he raced past him and into his own ship. The door shut and the ship at once vanished.

"Please, Doctor," the girl said, touching his arm. "Will you let me operate the controls? I can do it more quickly, rather than telling you—" She had already started into his ship; he followed mutely, letting her shut the door after them.

After a pause, Parsons said, "How is your mother?"

"You'll be seeing her," the girl said. "She's fine."

Parsons said, "You're Loris' children. From the future."

"Your children, too," the girl said. "Your son and daughter."

SEVENTEEN

As THE time ship moved into the future, Parsons understood at last why Loris had changed her mind. Why she had returned to Nova Albion for him, knowing that he had killed her father.

In the month that had followed, she had discovered that she was pregnant. Possibly she had even gone ahead into the future and seen their children. In any case, she had let the children be born; she had not had the zygotes removed and put covertly into the great Soul Cube, to merge with the hundreds of millions already there.

Realizing that, he felt a profound, humble emotion toward her, and, at the same time, pride.

"What's your brother's name?" he asked the girl. His daughter, he realized with a further deepening of emotion.

Grace said, "Nathan. She—our mother—wanted us to have names that you would approve of." She lifted her head and studied him. "Do you think we look like you? Would you have recognized us?"

"I don't know," he said. He was too overcome to think about it right now.

"We knew you," Grace said. "But of course we expected to see you; we knew that you came there, to do what had to be done. And we knew that you were unable to go through with it."

And so, he thought, you came back and did it for me.

Both of you. Aloud, he said, "How does your mother feel about what you did?"

"She understands that it's necessary. It would not have worked out, for her to have children by Corith. There was already too much interbreeding. She was aware of that, even in your time. But there did not seem to be any alternative, and the old lady—our great grandmother, Nixina—would not permit anything else. Of course in our time she's long since dead."

Parsons said, "Tell me why you have the caduceus emblem on your clothing."

"I'd rather wait," she said. "Until we get back. So we can all be there, my mother and my brother and you and I."

He thought, The family in its entirety.

"She told you about me?" he asked the girl.

"Oh, yes," she said. "All about you. We've waited a long time to see you face-to-face." Her even white teeth flashed as she smiled at him. Exactly as Loris had smiled at him, he thought.

History repeats itself, he thought. And this woman waiting year after year, all her life, until this moment: seeing her father for the first time. But, in contrast to Corith, I was not entombed in a transparent cube.

As he and his daughter stepped from the time ship, Loris came to meet them. Gray-haired, a handsome middle-aged woman . . . in her late fifties, he realized. Still the strong face, the erect posture. Her hand came out, and he saw the pleasure in her eyes, her dark, full eyes.

"The last time I saw you," she said huskily, "I cursed you. I'm sorry, Jim."

"I couldn't bring myself to do it," he said. "I got there, but that was all." He became silent then.

"For me, that was a long time ago," Loris said. "What do you think of our children?" She drew Grace over to her, and now, from the other ship, Nathan appeared. "They're almost nineteen," she said. "Don't they look healthy and sound?"

"Yes," he agreed tightly, surveying the three of

them. This is so much like *his* situation, he thought. If he had returned to life. His wife much older, his two children—which he did not even know he had. He said, "The combination of my racial heritage and yours makes an attractive amalgam.

"The union of the opposites," Loris said. "Come along, so we can sit down and talk. You can stay awhile, can't you? Before you go back to your own time?"

To my wife, he thought. How hard it is to reconcile that with this. With what I see here.

The Wolf Lodge did not seem to have changed in appearance in twenty years. The same dark, massive, aged beams. The wide stairs. The stone walls that had impressed him so much. This building would continue to stand a long, long time. The grounds, too, remained the same. The lawns and trees, the flower beds.

"Stenog remained in Drake's place for ten years or so," Loris said. "In case my father made a second try. Stenog had no way of telling what our circumstances were. He believed that Corith could still make an assassination attempt, but of course my father has been buried now for almost the full twenty years. We did not make any more attempts to revive him. Nixina died soon after our return from Nova Albion, and without her, much of the impetus dwindled away."

The power behind it all, Parsons thought. The savage, relentless schemes of a dried-up little old lady, who imagined herself as the protagonist of an ancient race reborn.

Loris said, "It was a fatal blow to us to discover that the man whom we had selected as the epitome of the conquering whites was actually a man from our own times. Born in our culture, adhering to its values. Stenog went back into time to protect our culture. That is, the aspect of our culture that he had taken the job of supporting. Our tribe, as you know, does not follow their system of birth or death." She added, "I have something to tell you about that, Jim."

Later, the four of them sat drinking coffee and facing one another.

"What is the caduceus?" Parsons asked. By now, he had begun to get an inkling.

His daughter said, "We're following in your footsteps, sir."

"That's right," Nathan said with agitation. "It's still illegal, but not for long—in another ten years we know it'll be accepted. We've looked ahead." His young face gleamed with pride and determination. Parsons saw some of the family's fanaticism, the desire to prevail at all costs. But in this boy, there was a fuller grasp on reality. He and his sister were not so far removed from the world as it actually was; the near-paranoid dreams were gone.

At least he hoped they were gone. Shifting his gaze, he studied Loris. The older Loris.

Can she manage them? he wondered. The image of the boy and girl at Corith's bedside remained in his mind. The swift act, completed in a matter of seconds; he had not been able to do it, and so they had, in his place. Because they believed that it had to be done. Possibly they were right. But—

"I'd like to know about your illegal group," he said, indicating the caducei.

With enthusiasm, the boy and girl spilled out their accounts, interrupting each other in their eagerness. Loris, silent, watched them with an expression that Parsons could not read.

They had, they told him, about a hundred and forty members in their profession (as they called it). Several had been caught by the government and exiled to the Martian prison colonies. The group distributed inflammatory propaganda, demanding the end of the euthanors and a resumption of natural birth—at the very least, the freedom of women to conceive and give birth, or to turn their zygote over to the Soul Cube if they preferred. The element of *choice*. And, as an essential, the end of enforced sterilization for the young men.

Breaking into her children's account, Loris said, "You understand that I'm still Mother Superior. I've been able to get a small number of males out of the hands of the sterilization agency . . . not many, but enough to give us hope."

Parsons thought, Maybe they have to be fanatics. In a world like this, where they're fighting compulsory sterilization, exile to prison camps without trial, vicious *shupos*. And, underneath it all, the ethos of death. A system devoted to the extinction of the individual, for the sake of the future.

Whatever virtues it might have, whatever good aspects—

"I guess there's no chance that you could stay here," Grace said. "With mother and us."

Awkwardly, Parsons said, "I don't know if you know it, but in my own time I have a wife." He felt his face flush, but neither of the children seemed embarrassed or surprised.

"We know," Nathan said. "We've gone back several times to have a look at you. Mother took us back when we were younger; we persuaded her to. Your wife seems very nice."

Loris said, in a practical tone, "Let's be realistic. Jim, at this point, is twenty years my junior." But something in her eyes, a certitude, made Parsons wonder what she was thinking.

Does she know something important about me? he asked himself. Something that I have no way of knowing? They have use of their time-travel equipment for any purpose that they want.

In a low voice, Loris said, "I know what makes you look so worried, Jim. You saw them kill my father. I want to tell you why they did it. You're afraid it's the maniacal fanaticism of the family showing itself in one more generation. You're wrong. They killed Corith to save your life. If he had lived, he would have had you destroyed; I knew it, and so did the children. They saw you unable to do it, and they admire you more. It was the highest morality possible. But your life is worth too much to them, to let anything happen to you. Their whole outlook is based on what I've told them about you, and what they've seen for themselves. You, with your system of values, your humane ethics, your sense of others, have formed them. And, through their profession, you will alter this society. Even if you yourself are not here."

None of them spoke, for a time.

"You were a powerful and unanswerable lesson for this society," Loris said.

To that, Parsons could say nothing.

Loris said, "And so was your profession."

"Thanks," he said finally.

The three of them smiled at him with great tenderness. And with love. My family, he said to himself. And, in these children, the best of both of us, of Loris and me.

"Do you want to go back to your own time now?" Loris said, in her considerate, mature manner.

He nodded. "I suppose I should."

Disappointment, crushing and bleak, appeared on the children's faces. But they said nothing. They accepted it.

Later on, Loris sent both Grace and Nathan off, so she and Parsons could be alone for a time.

"Will I ever be back here?" he asked her bluntly.

With composure, she said, "I won't tell you."

"But you know."

"Yes," she said.

"Why won't you tell me?"

"I don't want to rob you of the power of choosing for yourself. If I tell you, it will seem determined. Out of your hands. But of course, it would still be your choice—as it was your choice not to kill my father."

"Do you believe that choice actually exists? That it's not an illusion?"

She said, "I believe it's authentic."

He let it go at that.

"In one matter, however," she continued, "you have no choice. You know about that—what remains to be done. Of course, you can do it here as well as back in your own time."

"Yes," he said. "But I'd rather do it back there."

Rising, Loris said, "I'll take you back. Do you want to see the children again before you go?"

He hesitated, considering. "No," he decided. "I feel that I have to go back. And if I see them again, I probably won't."

Matter-of-factly, Loris said, "We've been without you for their lifetime. But for you, only an hour or so passed. If you decide to come back to us, it will follow a twenty year period for you. But—" She smiled. "For us, it will probably be during the next few days. You see?"

"You won't have to wait," he said.

Loris nodded.

"How strange," he said. "Having two families, at different periods in history."

"Do you consider that you have two? I see only one. Here, with the children. You have a wife back in your own time, but no family." Her eyes flared with the familiar determination.

Parsons said, "You would be a difficult person to live with." He spoke half-jokingly, but with more than a little seriousness.

"This is a difficult period in time," Loris said.

He could hardly argue that.

As they walked toward the time ship, Loris said, "Would you be afraid of the problems here? No, I know you wouldn't. There's no fear on your part. You would be a lot of help to us."

At the ship, as he shut the door after them, he said, "What about Helmar? Is he still around?"

Loris said, "He went over to the government, to join them."

That did not surprise him. "And Jepthe?"

"She's with us here. But in retirement. She's gotten quite feeble; in her old age she has none of Nixina's strength."

Presently she switched on the controls. He was on his way back, at last, to his own time.

"I'm afraid your car was wrecked," Loris said.

"When the dredge picked you up. We hadn't had the experience we needed then."

He said, "That's all right. I have insurance."

Once more, the highway with its educational signs. Cars moving toward San Francisco, and, on the other side, the traffic on its way to Los Angeles. He stood uncertainly on the shoulder of the road, smelling the oleander that the public roads department had planted, miles of it between the two strips. Then he began to walk.

Trudging along, wondering if any of the cars would stop—it meant unhooking from the automatic beam— he considered the work that lay ahead of him. He did not have to undertake it at once; in fact, he had years to accomplish it. Most of his lifetime.

He thought of his house, Mary standing on the front porch as he had last seen her. Image of her waving, pert and fresh in her green slacks . . . hair shining in the early-morning sunlight as he set off to his office.

How will I feel when I see her? he asked himself.

I wonder how soon I'll be going back into the future. A method of communicating with Loris had been arranged between them. How easy it would be . . .

A car slowed, left the lane, and coasted to a halt on the shoulder. "Engine trouble?" the driver called to him.

"Yes," he said. "I'd appreciate a ride into San Francisco."

A moment later he had gotten in; the car started up and rejoined the beam.

"Strange looking outfit you have on," the driver remarked politely, but with curiosity.

Parsons realized that he had come back to his time wearing clothes from another world entirely. And he had left his gray instrument case somewhere. This time it really was lost.

The ring of industrial installations around San Francisco appeared ahead. He watched the factories, tracks, towers and sheds go by beneath the highway.

I wonder where I can get the materials, he said to

himself. And where it should be placed. But evidently the placing was not a problem; he had found it, and that was what mattered. Can I do the work myself? he wondered. He had never done anything with stone before. Of course, the inscription itself was cut directly into the metal. Probably, after practice, he could manage it; he would not have to hire the job out.

If I can, he decided, I want to do it myself. To be sure there is no slip-up. After all, my life depends on it.

It would be interesting to see the plaque come into existence, here in his own time. Contrast to the eroded, damaged monument that had greeted him in the future, countless centuries hence . . .

But a job well done. And it had outlasted all his other acts in this world.

Maybe it should be buried, he decided. Sunk deep into the earth, out of sight. After all, it won't be needed for a long, long time.